영어로 읽는 세계 명작
Series

KB185972

Story of Frankenstein

53 프랑켄슈타인 이야기

Grade
5
1420 Words

YBM Si-sa

"They are prejudiced against me.
I am a good person and my life has been
harmless so far. In fact I have even done
some good. But a fatal prejudice clouds
their vision and while they should see a
friend, they see only a monster."

이 책을 펴내며

YBM 시사영어사에서는 '영어로 읽는 세계 명작 스프링 시리즈 30선'에 이어 '스프링 시리즈 추가 30선'을 개발하게 되어 '세계 명작 스프링 시리즈 60선'을 갖추게 되었습니다.

'세계 명작 스프링 시리즈 60선'은 세계적으로 가장 많이 읽히는 세계 명작 베스트 셀러만을 선정해 난이도를 6단계로 구분하여 중고 생들이 영어 습득 정도에 따라 알맞은 작품을 선택하여 읽을 수 있도록 한 학습 문고 시리즈입니다.

'세계 명작 스프링 시리즈 60선'은 영어를 모국어로 하는 원어민 전문 작가 수십 명에 의해 쓰여진 것으로, 깔끔하고 유려한 필치, 자연스러운 영어 表現 등이 돋보이는 작품으로, 읽는 이로 하여금 문학적 정서에 흠뻑 빠져들게 합니다. 또한 단어, 문법, 독해를 동시에 만족시킬 수 있는 자세한 단어 · 구문 해설, 내용의 이해를 묻는 Quiz, Chapter별 Comprehension Checkup, Word List 등을 실어 이야기를 읽는 재미 외에 논리적이고 창의적인 보조 학습이 가능하게 합니다. 뿐만 아니라 내용의 이해를 돕는 풍부한 상황 그림, 체재의 시각적 세련미는 독자들에게 읽는 재미를 더해 줍니다.

'세계 명작 스프링 시리즈 60선'이 여러분의 영어 능력 향상에 도움이 되기를 바랍니다.

YBM Si-sa 학습문고부

작가와 작품에 관하여

〈프랑켄슈타인 Frankenstein〉은 19세기 영국의 여류 소설가 메어리 셸리의 작품이다. 19세기 낭만주의 시대의 유명한 시인인 P. B. 셸리의 아내이기도 한 메어리 셸리는 스위스에 머무르는 동안 남편 셸리와 바이런(Byron)과의 대담, 또한 그 당시 유행한 괴기소설에서 자극을 받아 초인적인 능력을 갖춘 기괴한 형상의 거대한 인조인간을 다룬 〈프랑켄슈타인 Frankenstein〉(1818)을 발표했는데, 이 작품은 오늘날의 SF소설의 선구가 된 것으로 평가된다. 메어리 셸리의 또다른 작품으로는 전염병에 걸려서 인류가 단 한 사람만 남고 전멸하는 이야기인 〈마지막 사람 The Last Man〉(1826), 자전적인 작품인 〈로토어 Lodore〉(1835) 등이 있다.

생명의 탄생과 죽음에 관심을 갖고 무생물에 생명을 부여할 수 있는 방법을 알아낸 제네바의 과학자 프랑켄슈타인은 새로운 종을 탄생시키는 데 성공한다. 그러나 탄생된 생명체는 프랑켄슈타인의 기대와는 달리 끔찍한 괴물이었고 이에 놀란 프랑켄슈타인은 자신이 만들어낸 생명체에게서 도망쳐 버린다. 한편, 친구를 만들려는 시도를 계속하던 그 괴물은 자신의 외모에 대한 편견으로 사람들이 자신을 거부한다는 것을 알게 되고 깊은 절망감과 함께 자신을 외면해 버린 프랑켄슈타인에 대한 증오심을 불태운다. 프랑켄슈타인과 인간 전체에 대한 복수심에 가득 찬 괴물은 프랑켄슈타인이 사랑하는 가족과 친구들에게 차례차례 마수를 뻗치는데…

Contents

Frankenstein

생명의 탄생과 죽음에 깊은 관심을 가진 과학자로, 몇 년간의 연구 끝에 결국 생명체를 탄생시키는 데 성공하지만 자신이 만들어 낸 것이 다름 아닌 끔찍한 괴물임을 알고 그 생명체에 대한 어떠한 책임도 지지 않고 방기해 버린다.

The monster

프랑켄슈타인에 의해 창조된, 거구에 초인적인 힘을 가진 흉측한 몰골의 괴물. 친구를 원했지만 자신의 외모에 대한 편견으로 인해 사람들에게 거부당하자 자신을 만들어 낸 프랑켄슈타인과 인간 전체에 대한 적개심에 불타 잔인한 복수를 저지른다.

Walton

미지의 세계에 대한 탐험심에 불타는 선장으로, 북극으로의 탐험을 감행하던 도중에 괴물을 추격하다가 죽을 위기에 처한 프랑켄슈타인을 만나게 되어 그를 구해 준다. 프랑켄슈타인과 괴물에 얽힌 비극적인 이야기를 듣고 프랑켄슈타인을 동정하게 되는데...

Elizabeth

프랑켄슈타인이 사랑한 여인으로 그와 결혼한 바로 그 날 괴물에게 희생된다. 이 여인의 죽음으로 프랑켄슈타인은 극도로 상심하여 괴물에 대한 일생을 건 복수를 결심하고 필사의 추격전을 시작한다.

Chapter 1

St Petersburg, Dec 11th, 17-

My beloved sister Margaret,

You will be happy to know that I got here safely yesterday. I am writing to tell you that I am 5 already far north of London. I am very excited and feel the cold on my face. I am excited as I head toward the North Pole. I don't know what to expect.

It has been six years since I started on this 10 expedition. After making so many different trips I

really that think that I should do something great. I love the winter weather. The Russians travel in sleds and go more quickly and comfortably over the snow than the English stagecoaches do. I shall leave for the town of Archangel in two or three weeks. Once there, I will rent a ship and set sail for the North Pole in June. I don't know when, if ever, I will return.

---

expect 바라다, 기대하다
expedition [èkspədíʃən]
          탐험여행, 원정
sled 작은 썰매

quickly 신속하게
comfortably 편안하게
stagecoach 역마차, 합승마차
rent 빌리다, 세놓다

. . . .

7 I don't know what to expect.
  나는 무슨 일이 일어날지 예측할 수가 없구나.
9 It has been six years since I started on this
  expedition. 내가 이 탐험 여행을
  시작한 지도 어언 6년이 지났다.
7 I don't know when, if ever, I will
  return.
  만약 돌아간다면 그게
  언제가 될지는 모르겠구나.

Where does the speaker of the passage want to go? Answer in English.

ANS. To the North Pole

Archangel, March 28th, 17-

Time goes by very slowly when you are surrounded by frost and snow! I have rented a ship and have been busy hiring sailors for it. I am 5 excited about the trip, but I am very sad because I have not made any friends. Writing down my thoughts is a poor substitute for talking to a man who could sympathize with me.

There is no use complaining I suppose. I have 10 hired some of the crew. I am still excited about my voyage and I will leave as soon as the weather permits. Please write to me as often as you can. Your letters are a great comfort to me.

· ·

6 Writing down my thoughts is a poor substitute for talking to a man who could sympathize with me. (편지에) 내 생각들을 적어 보내는 것은 그나마 마음이 통하는 사람과 얘기하는 것을 조금은 대신할 수 있단다.

9 There is no use complaining 불평해 봤자 소용없는 일이다

11 as soon as the weather permits 날씨가 허락되면 곧

8 Not much has happened that is worth writing about (편지에) 쓸 만한 일들이 그다지 많이 일어나지는 않았다

July 7th, 17-

I am just writing you a few lines to say that I am now safely on my voyage. This letter will reach you by a merchant ship on its way to
5 Archangel. We are already very far north and although the weather is not as warm as in England, there is a warm southern breeze.

Not much has happened that is worth writing about, Margaret. But I am excited because I know
0 this will be a successful voyage.

surround 둘러싸다
frost 서리, 결빙
hire 고용하다
substitute [sʌ́bstitjùːt]
        대용물, 대리인
sympathize 동정하다, 공감하다
complain 불평하다
crew 선원, 승무원
voyage 항해, 선박여행
permit 허락하다
merchant 상인, 무역상인
successful 성공적인

이 글의 종류는?

① 수필
② 서간문
③ 기행문

1

August 5th, 17-

I have to tell you about something strange that happened.

Last Monday, we were surrounded by ice on all
5 sides and there was a very thick fog. We decided to stop until the weather cleared a bit. At about 2:00 the fog lifted and we saw a very strange sight. A low carriage attached to a sled drawn by dogs moved about a mile ahead of us to the north.
10 The driver of the sled looked like a man, but was gigantic. We watched through our telescopes until he was out of sight.

At dawn I saw the sailors on deck apparently talking to someone in the sea. A sled, like the one
15 we saw the night before, had drifted toward us. Only one dog remained alive and there was a man in the sled. The man was a European who asked me in English, "Before I come on board, please tell me where you are going."

carriage 탈것, 수레
attach 붙이다, 첨부하다
gigantic[dʒaigǽntik] 거대한
telescope 망원경
apparently 외견상, 명백하게
drift 표류하다

．．．．．．．．．．．．．．．．．．．．．．．

8 A low carriage attached to a sled drawn by dogs
   개가 끄는 썰매에 부착된 낮은 수레
11 until he was out of sight 그가 시야에서 안 보일 때까지
14 A sled, like the one we saw the night before, had
   drifted toward us. 우리가 지난 밤에 보았던 것과
   비슷한 썰매가 우리 쪽으로 떠내려왔다.

Whom did sailors see
through their telescopes?
Answer in English.

ANS. Someone who looked like a
man, but was gigantic.

3

I was surprised to hear such a question from a man who was almost dead. But I was even more surprised when I told him that we were going to the North Pole and he agreed to come on board! He was in very poor condition, but we slowly restored his health.

The crew was very curious about him and asked him many questions. When the lieutenant asked why he had come so far on such a strange craft, the man's face darkened as he replied, "To chase someone who ran away from me."

"If the man traveled in a sled like yours," said the lieutenant, "then we have seen him."

The stranger was quite excited when he heard this. Over the next few days his health has continued to improve, although he is uncomfortable around anyone but me.

I wrote earlier to you that I had no friends, but I seem to have found one in this stranger and I shall continue to record in my journal everything that happens between us.

restore (건강 따위를) 회복시키다
curious 알고 싶어하는,
　　　　호기심이 강한
lieutenant [lu:ténənt]
　　　　해군 대위, 부관
craft 선박
chase 뒤쫓다
journal 일기

. . . .

5 we slowly restored
　his health
　우리는 서서히 그의
　건강을 회복시켰다
12 If the man traveled in
　a sled like yours
　그 사람이 당신의 것과 비슷한
　썰매를 타고 여행을 했다면
16 although he is uncom-
　fortable around
　anyone but me
　나를 제외하고는 다른
　사람들과 어울리는 것을
　불편해하긴 했지만

낯선 이가 이 곳까지 오게 된 까닭
을 본문에서 찾아 영어로 쓰시오.

5

ANS. To chase someone who
ran away from him

August 13th 17-

My affection for the stranger gets stronger every day. He is feeling a lot better now and is always on deck looking for the sled. Although he 5 seems unhappy he often talks to me. He seemed sympathetic to my expedition, but when I told him that a man's life was a small price to pay for gaining knowledge, his face darkened. He spoke, "You unhappy man! Are you as mad as I am? I can 10 tell you my story, which I am sure will change your mind."

He spoke of once having a very noble friend, but then he had lost everything and could see no future for himself. I want to try to discover what 15 it is about him that makes him so much better than any person I have ever known.

· ·

7 a man's life was a small price to pay for gaining knowledge
지식을 얻기 위해 치러야 하는 대가치곤 인간의 삶은 하찮은 것에 불과하였다(지식을 얻기 위해서라면 인생도 걸 수 있다는 의미)

8 (I) offered to help any way I could
내가 할 수 있는 한 어떤 방법으로든 도움을 제공했다

12 in his own words as accurately as I can remember it
내가 기억할 수 있는 한 정확하게 그의 말 그대로

August 19th 17-

Yesterday the stranger said to me, "Captain Walton, I'm sure you understand that I have suffered a lot. I once thought that I would take these sufferings to my grave, but since you seek knowledge I will share them with you."

I told him how sorry I was that he had suffered and offered to help any way I could. He thanked me but said that nothing could change his fate. Then he said he would tell me his story the next day when I had free time. I have decided to write down everything he said in his own words as accurately as I can remember it. His story must be strange and frightening indeed!

affection 애정
knowledge 지식
suffer 고생하다
accurately 정확하게
frightening[fráitniŋ]
　　　무서운

According to the passage, the stranger must have been _____ a lot.

① happy
② suffering
③ traveling

ANS. ②

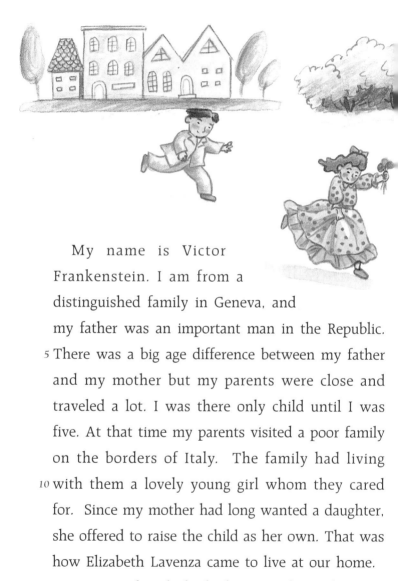

My name is Victor Frankenstein. I am from a distinguished family in Geneva, and my father was an important man in the Republic. 5 There was a big age difference between my father and my mother but my parents were close and traveled a lot. I was there only child until I was five. At that time my parents visited a poor family on the borders of Italy. The family had living 10 with them a lovely young girl whom they cared for. Since my mother had long wanted a daughter, she offered to raise the child as her own. That was how Elizabeth Lavenza came to live at our home.

Everyone loved Elizabeth. Once she said to me,

"Victor I will give you a present tomorrow." When she gave the gift to me I was so excited that I took it to be a promise of love. We called each 5 other cousins but she was more to me than a sister. I also had a close friend, named Henry Clerval. No one could have had a happier childhood than I did.

---

distinguished [distíŋgwiʃt]
유명한, 뛰어난
republic 공화국

difference 차이
border 국경지방, 경계
offer 제안하다, 제공하다

· ·

3 I was so excited that I took it to be a promise of love
나는 너무나 흥분해서 그것을 사랑의 증표로 받아들였어요
8 No one could have had a happier childhood than I
did. 나보다 더 행복한 어린 시절을 보낸 사람은 없을
것입니다.

Frankenstein과 직접적인 관련
이 없는 사람은?

① Elizabeth
② Henry
③ Margaret

ANS. ③

When I was 17 my parents wanted me to study at the university in Ingolstadt. My departure for school was delayed when Elizabeth caught scarlet fever. My mother caught it from her and died. When I finally was able to leave, I had a hard time saying goodbye to Henry and Elizabeth. Henry wanted to come with me but couldn't, and Elizabeth made me promise to write often.

At the school the first professor I met was M. Krempe. He was a rude man who told me that all my previous reading had been useless and I must start my studies over again. I had better luck when I met my chemistry professor, M. Waldman. He excited me very much with his talk of chemistry and how it was the branch of natural philosophy that held the greatest hope for the future. He took me into the laboratory and showed me all the machines and how they worked. From that day on, natural philosophy, and especially chemistry has been my only occupation.

---

departure 출발
delay 지연시키다, 미루다
previous 이전의
chemistry 화학

branch 부문, 분과
laboratory 실험실
occupation [àkjəpéiʃən]
　　　　　업무, 직업

. . . .

7 when Elizabeth caught scarlet fever
  엘리자베스가 성홍열에 걸렸을 때

10 I had a hard time saying goodbye
  나는 작별인사를 하기가 힘들었지요

20 how it was the branch of natural philosophy that held the greatest hope for the futune 어떻게 그것(화학)이 미래에 대한
  가장 위대한 희망을 주는 자연 철학의 한 분야가 되는지

I From that day on, natural philosophy, and especially chemistry has been my only occupation.
  그 날 이후로 줄곧 나는 자연 철학, 특히
  화학에만 몰두하게 되었습니다.

What has been Frankenstein's only occupation?

① chemistry
② biology
③ physics

ANS. 1

21

M. Waldman became a great friend and I spent two years studying very hard and didn't go home once. I was especially interested in the human body. I often asked myself where human life came 5 from. I watched dead bodies decay and I noticed living worms ate the dead. I was amazed how life and death depended on each other. I wondered, with so many great minds at this school, why I was the only one who noticed this. After many 10 days and nights of hard work, I was able to discover how to create life and bring lifeless forms to life.

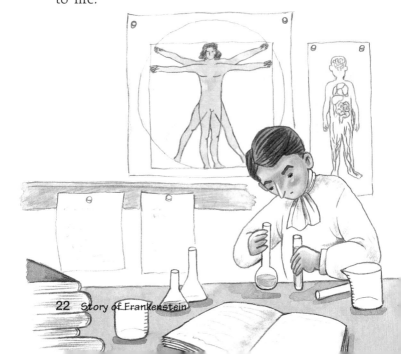

With such amazing power in my hands, I wondered how I could use it best. I decided to make a creature who was at least 8 feet tall. An entirely new species of beings would owe their existence to me. I spent all my time in the dissecting room and the slaughterhouse, gathering materials for my creation. Every night, I slaved to complete my task.

decay 썩다	slaughterhouse 도살장
notice 알아차리다	material 재료, 물질
amaze 놀라게 하다	slave 노예처럼[고되게] 일하다
dissect [disékt] 해부하다	complete 완성하다

6 I was amazed how life and death depended on each other.
나는 삶과 죽음이 얼마나 서로 밀접하게 관련되어 있는지에 놀랐습니다.

8 with so many great minds at this school, why I was the only one who noticed this
이 학교에는 그렇게 많은 석학이 있는데도 어떻게 나만이 그것을 알아차리게 되었는지

3 An entirely new species of beings would owe their existence to me.
완전히 새로운 종이 나로 인해 존재하게 되는 것입니다.

빈 칸에 알맞은 말을 본문에서 찾아 쓰시오.

Frankenstein tried to
_____ a new species.

ANS. create (또는 make)

It was a dark and dreary night in November when I had my first success. It was 1:00 AM when I first saw the yellow eye of the creature open. I had thought that the creature I had created was beautiful. But when it opened that eye, I was disgusted by it. The creature was ugly beyond all belief. I was horrified! I rushed out of the room in terror and collapsed on my bed.

I suddenly awoke to find the monster standing next to me and reaching out toward me. No one could imagine the horror of that face! It might have spoken, but I didn't hear. It tried to stop me but I rushed downstairs, outside and hid in the courtyard.

In the damp, cool morning I walked until I

came to an inn. I saw a carriage coming toward the inn, and out of the carriage popped Henry Clerval. "My dear Frankenstein," he exclaimed, "how lucky to meet you at this moment!"

5   I was delighted to see him and I begged him to give me news of my father, brothers and Elizabeth.

---

dreary[dríəri] 황량한
horrify 무섭게 하다
terror 공포, 겁
collapse 맥없이 쓰러지다

horror 공포, 전율
damp 습기 있는, 축축한
pop 갑자기 나오다, 갑자기 움직이다
delighted 아주 기뻐하는

. . . .

10 I was disgusted by it 그것은 혐오스러울 지경이었어요
11 The creature was ugly beyond all belief.
    그 생명체는 믿을 수 없을 만큼 추했습니다.
16 I suddenly awoke to find the monster standing next to me
    and reaching out toward me. 나는 불현듯 깨어나서 괴물이
    내 옆에 서 있다가 내쪽으로 손을 뻗치고 있는 것을 보았습니다.
18 It might have spoken 그것이 말을 했을지도 모릅니다

How was the creature
Frankenstein gave life to?

① dreary
② ugly
③ damp

ANS. ②

"They are all very well and happy," replied Clerval, "but they are a little worried that they don't hear from you very often. And now that I see you, you look a little sick—as if you have been awake for several nights."

"You have guessed right. I have been very busy, but I think my work is finished now and I shall be able to get some rest," I said. "Let's go home." I didn't dare to tell Henry what had happened the previous night.

I was then terrified that the creature I left in my apartment might still be there, but even more frightened that Henry might see it. I asked Henry to wait at the bottom of the stairs while I went up. I was greatly relieved to find that my room was empty and the creature had left. I went back down to invite Clerval inside.

I was so delighted that the monster had gone. I jumped over chairs and hugged Henry, clapped my hands and laughed out loud. Henry at first thought this was my reaction to seeing him again. But he saw the wild look in my eye and couldn't account for my uncontrollable laughter.

"My dear Victor," he cried, "for God's sake, what is wrong? Don't laugh like that. You are really sick. What caused this?"

5 "Don't ask me," I said covering my eyes. I thought I saw the monster in front of me. "Save me! Save me!" I cried as I imagined the monster grabbing me. I fell down to the floor in a fit.

....

worried 걱정하는
terrify [térəfài] 놀라게 하다
relieve 안도케 하다
hug 포옹하다, 껴안다
clap (손뼉을) 치다

reaction 반응
account (…의 이유를) 밝히다(for)
uncontrollable 제어할 수 없는
grab 움켜쥐다, 붙잡다
fit (병의) 발작, 까무러침

....

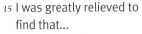

4 as if you have been awake for several nights
  며칠 밤을 꼬박 지새운 사람처럼
8 I didn't dare to tell Henry what had happened
  나는 감히 헨리에게 무슨 일이 있었는지 말을 할 수가
  없었어요
15 I was greatly relieved to
  find that...
  …한 것을 발견하고는 크게
  안도했지요

Where are they now?

① at the university
② in Frankenstein's
  apartment
③ in Henry's apartment

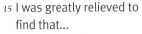

27

ANS. ②

That was the beginning of a nervous fever that held me for several months. During that time, Henry was my only nurse. Realizing that my father was old and Elizabeth would be really upset to see
5 me in this condition, he hid my illness from them. I was really quite sick and constantly saw the horrible monster in front of me. Slowly, however, I got better–although I occasionally upset my friend by falling into fits again. I knew I had
10 finally recovered when I noticed that it was spring.

"Henry," I said, "you have been so very kind to me by spending the entire winter nursing me. How can I ever repay you?"

"You can repay me by writing a letter to your father and cousin," replied Henry. "They are very worried because they haven't heard from you in so long. I have a letter for you. I think it's from Elizabeth."

Elizabeth's letter was quite long. She wrote of how kind Henry had been and of how much my family missed me. She wrote also of her dear friend, Justine Moritz, and of my youngest brother, William, whom everyone seemed to love. I decided to answer Elizabeth's letter right away.

---

nervous 신경성의
upset 당황케 하다
illness 질병
constantly 지속적으로

horrible 무서운, 소름끼치는
occasionally[əkéiʒənəli] 때때로
recover 회복하다
repay(-repaid-repaid) 보답하다

3 Realizing that…, he hid my illness from them.
…을 알았기에 그는 내 병을 그들에게
말하지 않았지요.

12 by spending the entire winter
nursing me 겨울 내내
나를 간호함으로써

What was wrong with Frankenstein?

① He fell ill.
② He was very proud of his creature.
③ He hated to see his family.

ANS. ①

I

Comprehension Checkup

1. 지금까지의 내용을 가장 적절하게 요약한 것은?

① The birth of the monster

② Frankenstein as a scientist

③ The girl whom Frankenstein loved

2. Who is Frankenstein?

① 괴물의 본명

② 괴물을 발명한 과학자의 이름

③ 괴물이 태어난 지역의 이름

3. 괴물에 대한 묘사로 옳지 <u>않은</u> 것은?

① gigantic   ② ugly   ③ friendly

4. 등장 인물의 성품에 대한 연결로 바르지 <u>않은</u> 것은?

① Frankenstein - passionate

② Walton - warm-hearted

③ Henry - selfish

5. Walton 선장이 Frankenstein을 처음 만났을
때의 상황으로 옳지 <u>않은</u> 것은?

① Frankenstein은 괴물을 추적하는 중이었다.
② Frankenstein의 건강 상태는 좋지 않았다.
③ Walton의 배는 남극으로 향하고 있었다.

6. 괴물이 탄생된 순간 Frankenstein 박사가 보인 반응은?

① horrified   ② bored   ③ satisfied

7. Frankenstein에 대한 설명으로 옳지 <u>않은</u> 것은?

① He is from Geneva.
② He had a very unfortunate childhood.
③ He was fascinated by natural philosophy.

8. 등장 인물과 그 사람에 대한 설명을 바르게 연결하시오.

① Walton   •   • ⓐ met Frankenstein while
                             sailing to the north.

② Frankenstein •   • ⓑ came to Frankenstein's
                             and lived with his family.

③ The monster •   • ⓒ created a monster.

④ Elizabeth   •   • ⓓ was a creature made by
                             Frankenstein.

정답은 p.128에

Chapter 2

One evening several months later when Henry and I returned home, I found the following letter from my father:

My Dear Victor,

5   I am writing to tell you the terribly sad news that your brother, William, is dead. It appears that he was murdered. Elizabeth is in deep, deep shock. Please come home now, Victor, because only you can make her feel better.

10   Your affectionate and grieving father,
                                    Alphonses Frankenstein

Henry saw my face sadden as I read the letter. I told him I intended to go home at once, and he agreed to go with me. The journey home was
15 depressing. I had not been home to Geneva for six

years. Before we reached the city, I decided that I should visit the spot where my poor William was murdered.

terribly 몹시, 무섭게
murder 살해하다
affectionate [əfékʃənit]
　　　　　애정이 깊은
grieve 몹시 슬퍼하다, 상심하다
sadden 슬퍼지다
intend …할 작정이다
journey 여행, 여정
depressing 우울한, 울적해지는

． ．

6 It appears that he was murdered.
그는 살해당한 것 같구나.
4 the spot where my poor
William was murdered
불쌍한 나의 (동생) 윌리엄이
살해된 장소

How long has Frankenstein
been away from home?

① several months
② six years
③ several weeks

3

ANS. ②

As I neared the spot a violent, yet beautiful thunderstorm began. I clasped my hands together, looked toward 5 heaven and said, "My dear William, this is your funeral!"

Suddenly I saw a large figure hiding in a clump of trees in front of me. I froze and stared intently. I was not mistaken. As the 1 lightening flashed I saw it clearly. It was the wretch, the filthy demon to whom I had given life!

Why was he there? Was he my brother's murderer? The instant the idea crossed my mind, I knew it was true. I shook and leaned against a 1

tree for support. The figure moved quickly and I lost it in the darkness. No human could have killed so fair a child. He was the murderer. I thought about chasing him, but another flash of
5 lightening showed that he was already too far away to chase.

I entered my father's house at about five. Everyone was in deep sorrow. "Elizabeth really needs to be consoled," my brother Ernest said.
10 "She blames herself for the murder. But since the murderer has been discovered..."

---

figure 형상, 인물, 모양
clump 수풀, 덤불
intently 열심히, 오로지

wretch 비열한 사람
filthy [fílθi] 추악한, 불결한
console 위로하다

• •

10 I was not mistaken. 내가 잘못 봤을 리가 없었어요.
11 It was the wretch, the filthy demon to whom
I had given life! 그것은 내가 생명을
주었던 놈, 그 추악한 악마가
아니겠습니까!
2 No human could have
killed so fair a child.
인간이라면 그렇게
순진한 아이를
죽였을 리가 없지요.

Quiz

Who does Frankenstein
think murdered William?
Answer in Korean.

"The murderer has been discovered? Good God, how can that be? It is impossible to catch him. I saw him last night and he flies like the wind."

"I don't know what you mean," replied Ernest
5 with wonder, "but to us the discovery of the murderer makes us even more miserable. No one believed it at first—especially Elizabeth—but there is no doubt that Justine Moritz is the killer."

"She is accused? But that is wrong. Surely
10 everyone knows that, Ernest."

Ernest told me that on the morning my brother was killed, a servant discovered a picture of my mother in her pocket. She went instantly to the magistrate and Justine was arrested that day.

15 This strange tale did not shake my faith. "You are mistaken. I know the murderer. Justine is innocent."

At that moment my father and Elizabeth entered the room. They were happy that I believed Justine to be innocent while everyone else thought she was guilty. We all passed a few sad hours
5 together until eleven o'clock when we headed to the courthouse for Justine's trial.

discovery 발견
miserable 비참한
accuse 고소하다
magistrate [mǽdʒəstrèit]
    치안 판사, 행정 장관
arrest 체포하다
trial 재판

....

1 Good God, how can that be? 맙소사, 어떻게 그럴 수가 있지?
5 the discovery of the murderer makes us even more
   miserable 살인범이 누구인지 알고 나서 우리는
   한층 더 비참함을 느꼈어요
15 This strange tale did not shake my faith.
   이 이상한 얘기도 내 믿음을
   흔들어 놓지는 못했습니다.

Who was accused of
murdering William?

① Ernest
② Elizabeth
③ Justine

ANS.③

Justine seemed calm and confident of her innocence. Several witnesses were called against her. She was out the entire night that William was murdered. A market woman, who had asked her
5 what she was doing, saw her near the murder spot. She had seemed dazed by the question. Justine had returned home at about eight o'clock. When asked where she had been, she replied that she had been looking for William. When she was
10 shown the body she became hysterical and had to be confined to bed. Horror filled the courtroom when Elizabeth said that the picture found on her was one she had given William on the day of his murder.

15　　In her defense, Justine said that she had been greatly disturbed by William's disappearance and looked for him outside the city gates. However she didn't get back to the city before the gates closed and was forced to spend the night outside. She
20 had gone by the murder spot by accident. The market woman's question surprised her because she had been awake all night. She didn't know

how she got the picture. She could only speculate that the real murderer placed it there.

Several character witnesses were called in her defense, but they were rather timid in their
5 testimony since they actually believed she was guilty.

---

confident 자신감이 있는
innocence 무죄, 결백
witness 목격자, 증인
daze 멍하게 하다, 현혹시키다
hysterical 병적으로 흥분한,
　　　　　히스테리의
confine 감금하다, 제한하다

defense 변호, 항변
disturb 마음을 어지럽게 하다
disappearance 실종, 사라짐
speculate [spékjəlèit]
　　　　　추측하다, 사색하다
timid 소심한, 두려워하는
testimony 증언

· ·

2 Several witnesses were called against her.
　몇 명의 증인이 소환되어 그녀에게 불리한 증언을 했어요.
19 She had gone by the murder spot by
　accident. 그녀는 우연히 살인이 일어난
　장소 옆을 지나가게 되었습니다.
5 since they actually
　believed she was guilty
　그들은 그녀가 실제로
　유죄라고 믿었기 때문에

Justine이 살인범으로 지목받게
된 결정적인 이유를 우리말로 간단
히 설명하시오.

I believed in her innocence; I knew of it. Could that hellish demon I created have placed the picture in her pocket just for fun? I could tell by the mood of the courtroom and the faces of the judges that they did not believe Justine was innocent. I rushed from the courtroom in agony.

The next day when I returned to the courtroom, I was utterly shocked to learn that Justine had confessed. When I returned home, Elizabeth insisted on visiting Justine so I went

with her to the prison where Justine was kept.

Justine stood when we entered and then fell, weeping, at my cousin's feet. My cousin wept too. "Oh, Justine!" she said. "Why did you rob me of my last consolation?"

"Do you also believe me to be evil?"

replied Justine crying bitterly. "Are you joining with my enemies to crush me—to condemn me as a murderer?"

"Get up, my dear girl," said Elizabet. "Why are
5 you kneeling if you are innocent? I believed you were innocent until I heard that you had confessed."

hellish 흉악한, 소름끼치는	insist 고집하다, 주장하다
courtroom 법정	consolation 위안(이 되는 것)
agony[ǽgəni] 고통	evil 사악한
utterly 아주, 완전히	condemn 비난하다, 유죄 판결을 내리다
confess 자백하다	kneel(-knelt-knelt) 무릎을 꿇다

6 I rushed from the courtroom in agony.
나는 괴로워하며 서둘러 법정을 빠져나왔습니다.
10 Elizabeth insisted on visiting Justine
엘리자베스는 저스틴에게 가보겠다고 고집을 부렸지요
17 Why did you rob me of my last consolation?
너는 어째서 내 마지막 희망마저 앗아가 버렸니?

본문에 나타난 Frankenstein의 심리 상태로 적절치 않은 것은?

① miserable
② bored
③ shocked

ANS. ②

"I confessed to a lie, so that I could obtain absolution," Justine paused, weeping and then continued; "I loved William very much and now I shall soon see him in heaven."

5   During this conversation I stood in the corner of the room. The two women wept bitterly and tried to console one another. Justine said she was not afraid to die. But the poor victim who was to die the next day could not feel such agony as I 10 did! She knew she was innocent, while I knew I was guilty of creating an unspeakably horrible, murdering monster.

    The next day Justine was executed as a murderess. From the tortures of my own heart, I 15 turned to think about the deep grief of Elizabeth and of my father's sorrow—all this was my fault! I saw those I loved spend so much sorrow on the graves of William and Justine, the first victims of my evil practices.

20   I was deeply saddened by these events. Justine died and she was at peace while I was still alive and tortured by what I had brought about. I wept

daily. Elizabeth tried to comfort me. But since she did not know my dark secret, her words had little effect on me. I left my home and seek peace in the calm
5 setting of the Alps, near Mont Blanc.

absolution 면제, 사면
unspeakably 말할 수 없이
execute [éksikjùːt]
　　　　사형을 집행하다
murderess 살인자(여성형)
torture 고통; 고문하다, 괴롭히다
practice 실행, 실시
comfort 위로하다

．．．．．．．．．．．．．．．．．．．．．．．

8 But the poor victim who was to die the next day could not feel such agony as I did!
하지만 다음 날 사형이 집행될 예정인 그 불쌍한
희생자도 나만큼 괴롭지는 않았을 거예요!

17 I saw those I loved spend so much sorrow
나는 내가 사랑하는 사람들이 그토록 큰 슬픔을
겪는 것을 보았습니다

What happened to
Justine?

① She was executed.
② She was set free.
③ She was put into prison.

43

One day, although rain and mist hid the peaks I decided to go on a mountain climb. I thought that the tranquility or the solitude of the mountain was worth the trouble. It was nearly noon when I reached top of my ascent. I was awed by the beauty and prayed to the mountain spirits to either allow me this brief happiness or take me away from all life's cares.

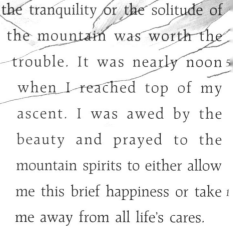

Suddenly I saw the figure of a man in the distance heading toward me at superhuman speed. He bounded over the cracks and crevices that only a little earlier I had crossed with such great caution. As he came closer, I saw that it was the wretch whom I had created! I shook with rage and horror. He approached; his face looked full of anguish combined with hatred and evil. I hardly noticed this. Rage and hatred first left me unable to speak but I recovered to pour my fury and contempt on him.

"Devil," I exclaimed, "how dare you approach me! Don't you fear my vengeance coming down on your miserable head? Get out of here you vile insect! Or rather, stay so that I can kick you to death!"

tranquility 고요함	exceed 초과하다
solitude 고독, 외로움	rage 분노
awe …에게 두려운 마음이 들게 하다	anguish[ǽŋgwiʃ] 고뇌
	combine 결합시키다
bound 뛰다, 튀다	fury 격노, 격분
crack 갈라진 금, 틈	contempt 경멸
crevice 갈라진 틈, 균열	vengeance 복수심
caution 주의, 조심	vile 혐오할 만한, 비열한

· ·

9 either allow me this brief happiness or take me away from all life's cares 나에게 이 짧은 행복을 허락하시든지, 아니면 삶의 모든 걱정거리들을 가져가시든지

15 He bounded over the cracks and crevices that only a little earlier I had crossed with such great caution. 바로 조금 전에 내가 그렇게 도 조심스럽게 건너왔던 협곡들을 그는 깡충 뛰어넘었지요.

4 so that I can kick you to death 내가 너를 죽음으로 몰아넣을 수 있도록

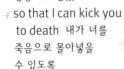

Frankenstein과 괴물이 서로에 게 갖는 공통적인 감정은?

① hatred

② satisfaction

③ curiosity

ANS. 1

"I expected this reception," said the demon. "Every man hates what is wretched. How much I must be hated! You, my creator, despise and reject me and want to kill me. How dare you play with
5 life like that! Do your duty towards me and I will do mine to you. If you agree to my request, I will leave you and the rest of humanity alone. If you refuse, I will slaughter everyone who crosses my path."

10   "Wretched monster! The tortures of hell are too mild for you. Come closer so I can take the life that I so mistakenly created."

I sprang toward the monster but he easily escaped me and said, "Calm down and listen to
15 what I have to say. Remember that I am your creature. Make me happy and I will be good. Listen to me, Frankenstein. You accuse me of murder, yet you want to murder what you created. Come with me to the cabin on the top of the
20 mountain and listen to my long and strange tale."

As he said this he led the way across the lake. I thought he was my brother's murderer and I wanted either a confirmation or a denial. For the first time I felt some responsibility toward my creation. We reached the cabin and the monster began to tell his story.

reception 응접, 접대	slaughter[slɔ́ːtər] 죽이다
wretched 비참한, 불쌍한	torture 심한 고통
despise 멸시하다	mistakenly 잘못하여
reject 거부하다	confirmation 확인
duty 의무	denial 부인
humanity 인류	responsibility 책임감

. . . .

4 How dare you play with life like that!
어떻게 당신은 생명을 가지고 그렇게 장난을 칠 수 있는가!
8 I will slaughter everyone who crosses my path
나는 내 곁을 지나는 모든 사람들을 죽일 테다.
11 so I can take the life that I so mistakenly created
내가 실수로 만들어낸 생명을 다시 빼앗을 수 있도록
17 You accuse me of murder, yet you want to murder what you created. 당신은 나더러 살인자라고 하면서 자기가 창조한 것을 죽이려 하고 있소.

이 본문의 바로 다음에 이어질 내용으로 가장 알맞은 것은?

① Frankenstein의 변명
② 괴물이 그 동안 겪은 이야기
③ Frankenstein과 괴물의 격투 장면

ANS. ②

"It is hard for me to remember my early days. When I first left your cottage I took some clothes but they were not enough to keep me warm. I slowly and painfully learned to distinguish all the
5 sensations of the body–cold, heat, light, dark and so on. I had to look for food and soon learned what was edible and inedible. I wandered far and wide and eventually found a hut that I could occupy undisturbed.

10 "Not too far from my hovel was a small cottage. One day I saw that a family which consisted of a young woman, a young man and an old man who made music on a guitar lived in the cottage. The music was the sweetest sound I ever heard. I

observed over the next few days that the young man went out to work in the daytime and the young woman stayed home and worked in the house. I soon understood that the old man was blind and spent the days playing his guitar.

"They were not entirely happy. Occasionally the woman and the man went apart and wept. I didn't know why they were unhappy until I noticed that they did not always have enough to eat. I wanted to help them and I found a way that I could."

distinguish 구별하다   undisturbed [ʌ̀ndistə́:rbd]
sensation 감각, 지각   방해받지 않는
edible 먹을 수 있는   hovel 광, 헛간
occupy 차지하다   observe 관찰하다

. . . .

8 a hut that I could occupy undisturbed
  내가 방해받지 않고 차지할 수 있는 오두막
13 The music was the sweetest
  sound I ever heard.
  그 음악은 내가 지금껏
  들어본 것 중 가장
  아름다운 소리였지.

Where did the monster stay?

① in a hut
② in a family's cottage
③ in Frankenstgein's
    apartment

9

ANS.①

"At night I took the young man's tools and chopped wood for the following day. They were
5 greatly astonished and I spent the winter observing them. I learned that they could communicate
10 with each other by making sounds. They called each other 'Agatha' or 'Felix' or 'father' or 'brother' or 'sister.' How I wanted to talk to them!

"The seasons changed and soon it was a full year since I was created. By daily observation of
15 the family, I managed to understand their language. Felix's fiancee came to live with them and he was much happier than he had been before.

"One day before winter set in, Felix and the
20 two women went for a walk and left the old man alone. I decided that this was the moment of truth. I approached the cottage door.

"I knocked. 'Who's there?' said the old man. 'Come in.'

"I entered. 'I'm sorry to bother you, but I am a traveler in this part of the country and would be
5 grateful if I could rest by your fire for a little while.'

"'Enter,' said the old man, 'and I will do what I can. But I am blind and my children are far from home, so I can't prepare food for you.'"

---

chop 자르다, 딱딱 찍다   observation[àbzərvéiʃən] 관찰
astonish 놀라게 하다   grateful 감사하고 있는, 고마워하는
communicate 의사소통 하다   prepare 준비하다, 마련하다

· ·

13 it was a full year since I was created
    내가 만들어진 이래로 만 일년이 지났다
4 (I) would be grateful if I could rest by your fire
   for a little while 제가 불 옆에서
   잠시 쉴 수 있다면 감사하겠습니다

빈 칸에 알맞은 말을 본문에서 찾
아 쓰시오.

The monster understood
their _____ by
observing them.

"'Don't worry, my kind friend. I have food. It is only a little rest and warmth that I want.'

"He thought by my accent that I was French. I told him that I was a friendless man who was in the area to seek a family I knew of, but had never seen.'

"'Don't worry,' he said, 'it is a sad thing to be friendless, but kind people are all about us. I am sure that the family you seek will welcome you with open arms.'

"'They are kind people all right. But they are prejudiced against me. I am a good person and my life has been harmless so far. In fact I have even done some good. But a fatal prejudice clouds their vision and while they should see a friend, they see only a monster.'

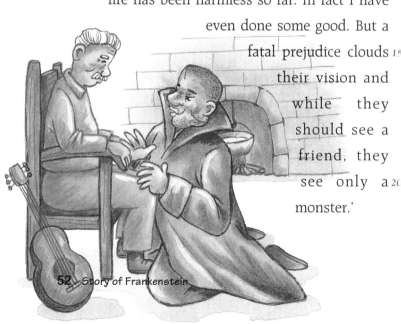

"'Where do these people live?'

"'Near here.'

"The old man paused and then continued, 'If you will tell me your story, I may be able to help you to convince them of your goodness. Even if you were a criminal I would help. My family and I have been condemned, although we are innocent. So judge for yourself if I can understand your situation.'"

---

prejudiced[prédʒədist] 편견을 가진　convince 납득시키다
harmless 해가 없는, 악의 없는　criminal 범죄자
fatal 치명적인, 운명의　condemn 비난하다

. . . .

5 to seek a family I knew of, but had never seen
내가 알고는 있지만, 전혀 만나본 적이 없는 가족을 찾기 위해

14 a fatal prejudice clouds their vision
치명적인 편견이 그들의 시야를 가리지요

4 I may be able to help to convince them of
your goodness 제가 그들에게 당신의
선함을 납득시키는 데 도움을 줄 수
있을지도 모릅니다.

본문의 내용과 일치하면 T, 일치하
지 않으면 F를 쓰시오.

( ) The old man is blind.
( ) The monster wants to
kill the old man.

ANS. T, F

"'How can I thank you? You have spoken the first words of kindness to me. Your humanity assures me of success with those friends I shall soon meet.'

5 "'May I know that names of those friends and where they live?'

"I paused. This was the moment of decision. It would either rob me of, or give me happiness forever. I fell back into a chair and sobbed. At that 10 moment I heard the approaching footsteps of the young people. I cried, 'Now is the time! Save and protect me! You and your family are the friends I seek. Don't desert me now!'

"'Good God!' exclaimed the old man. 'Who are 15 you?'

"At that moment the cottage door opened and in came Felix and the two women. Who can describe their horror at seeing me? One woman fainted and the other rushed from the cottage. 20 Felix charged forward and tore me away from his father. In a fury he hurled me to the ground and beat me with a stick."

assure 보장하다, 확실하게 하다   exclaim 소리치다
decision 결정, 결심   faint 기절하다
sob 흐느끼다   charge 돌진하다
desert[dizə́:rt] 버리다   hurl 집어던지다, 세게 던지다

. . . .

7 It would either rob me of, or give me happiness
  forever. 그것은 내게서 행복을 영원히 빼앗아갈
  수도 있고, 영원히 보장해 줄 수도 있었지.

17 Who can describe their horror at
  seeing me? 나를 보았을 때
  그들이 느꼈을 공포를 누가
  상상이나 할 수 있을까?

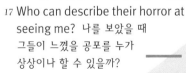

괴물을 보고서 오두막의 가족들이
보인 반응이 아닌 것은?

① 기절했다.
② 도망쳤다.
③ 살려 달라고 애걸했다.

ANS.③

"I could have ripped him apart but my heart was too heavy. When I saw he was about to hit me again, in pain and anguish I fled from the cottage to my hovel.

5 "Cursed, cursed creature! Why did I live? Why didn't I kill myself then and there? I don't know. There was no person on earth who would pity or help me. No, from that moment on I declared everlasting war on human beings—and the greatest 10 of all my enemies would be you, who made me and sent me out into this misery.

"I spent the night in the forest. When I returned to my hovel in the morning, I went to the cottage and saw that it was abandoned. I 15 returned to my hovel and spent the day in utter and stupid despair. The thought of my friends' tears soothed me. When I thought of how they had rejected me, anger returned. As soon as night fell, I returned to the cottage and set it on fire. I 20 was delighted watching it burn completely."

rip 쪼개다, 찢다	misery 비참한 신세, 불행
flee(-fled-fled) 도망치다	abandon 버리다
cursed 저주를 받은, 저주할 만한	despair 절망, 자포자기
declare 선언하다, 단언하다	soothe[suːð] 위로하다
everlasting 영원한	completely 완전히

....

1 I could have ripped him apart
그를 갈기갈기 찢어 놓을 수도 있었어

7 There was no person on earth who would pity or help me.
이 세상에는 나를 불쌍히 여기거나 도와 주는 사람이 아무도 없었다.

8 from that moment on 그 순간부터 줄곧

18 As soon as night fell 밤이 되자마자

19 I was delighted watching burn completely.
나는 (그것이) 완전히 타버리는 것을 보면서 기뻐했지.

괴물은 궁극적으로 누구를 원망하고 있는가?

① Frankenstein
② himself
③ Felix

ANS. ①

57

"I was not sure what to do next until my thoughts turned to you. I knew you were from Geneva. I felt only hatred for you. You had created me with feelings and passions and then tossed me out into the world alone. I was determined to seek 5 justice from you.

"My travels were long and difficult. I went out during the day once and I saw a young girl playfully running from a young man. She ran along the bank of a stream when suddenly she 10 slipped into the rapid stream. I rushed from my hiding place. Although the river current was strong, with a great effort I managed to save her. She was unconscious and I tried hard to revive her. Suddenly the man she had been fleeing from 15 interrupted me. He snatched her from my arms and fled into the forest. I don't know why, but I followed. When he saw me he fired a gun at me. I fell to the ground and he sped off deeper into the forest. 20

"This was the reward for my kindness! I vowed eternal hatred and vengeance on all mankind."

passion 열정
toss 내팽개치다, 던지다
playfully 명랑하게
slip 미끄러지다
current 조류, 물살
unconscious 무의식의
flee(-fled-fled) 달아나다
interrupt[ìntərʌ́pt]
    가로막다, 저지하다
snatch 낚아채다
speed(-sped-sped)
    급히 가다
vow 맹세하다
eternal 영원한

. . . .

1 I was not sure what to do next until my thoughts turned to
you. 당신을 떠올리고서야 나는 비로소 무엇을 해야 할지 확신이 섰소.

3 You had created me with feelings and passions and then
tossed me out into the world alone. 당신은 나를 감정과 열정을
가진 존재로 만들어 놓고서는 홀로 세상 밖으로 던져 버렸지.

5 I was determined to seek justice from you.
난 당신에게 공정한 심판을 내리기로 결심했소.

9 She ran along the bank of a stream when
suddenly she slipped into the rapid stream.
그녀는 시냇가를 따라 달리다가 갑자기
미끄러져 급류에 휩쓸렸지.

"I was not sure what to do
next until my thoughts
turned to you."에서 밑줄 친 부
분이 의미하는 것은?

① 복수   ② 자살   ③ 여행

ANS. 1

"Soon I came close to Geneva. One day while I was sleeping a beautiful, innocent child disturbed me. The idea came to me that this child was unprejudiced and was too young to be afraid of 5 deformity. If I could seize him and educate him as my friend and companion, I would not be so lonely.

"Urged by this impulse I grabbed the boy as he passed. As soon as he saw my face he screamed. I 10 put my hand over his mouth and said, 'Child, I don't want to hurt you. Listen to me.'

"He struggled violently. 'Let me go,' he cried; 'Monster! Ugly wretch! You wish to eat me and tear me to pieces. You are an ogre. Let me go, or I 15 will tell my papa.'

"'Boy, you will never see your papa again. You must come with me.'

"'Hideous monster! Let me go. My papa is M. Frankenstein. He is an important man and he will
5 punish you. You don't dare keep me.'

"'Frankenstein! Then you belong to my enemy. You will be my first victim.'"

---

deformity 기형, 보기 흉함
companion 동료, 친구
urge 권장하다, 촉구하다
impulse 충동
struggle 몸부림치다

violently 격렬하게
ogre[óugər] 사람을 잡아먹는
　　도깨비, 무섭고 잔인한 사람
hideous 무시무시한, 소름끼치는
punish 처벌하다

· ·

4 (this child) was too young to be afraid of deformity
그 아이는 기형을 두려워하기에는 아직 너무 어렸지

5 If I could seize him and educate him as my friend
내가 그를 붙잡아 내 친구가 되도록 교육시킨다면

8 Urged by this impulse 이러한 충동에 사로잡혀

14 Let me go, or I will tell my papa.
날 보내주세요. 그렇지 않으면
우리 아빠한테 이를 거예요.

아이가 괴물에게 보인 반응으로 알
맞은 것은?

① frightened
② pleased
③ excited

ANS. ①

"The child still struggled and cursed me. I grabbed his throat to silence him and in a moment he lay dead at my feet. As I gazed on him my heart swelled with hellish triumph. I exclaimed, 'I too can create destruction. This death will cause my enemy despair and a thousand other miseries will torment and destroy him.'

"As I looked at the child's lifeless body, I noticed he carried a picture of a woman. I took the picture and headed off to find a hiding place. Entering a barn that I thought was deserted, I saw a young woman sleeping. At first I thought I should wake her, but then realized that she too would curse me. The idea was madness, but it stirred a demon inside of me. She, not I, would suffer for the murder I committed! I took the picture and placed it inside her dress.

"For several days I haunted the spot of the murder, sometimes wishing to see you. I eventually came to this spot and you and I will not leave until you agree to my request. I am alone
5 and miserable in the world. But someone as deformed and horrible as myself could not deny herself to me. My companion must be the same species as me and have the same defects. You must create this being."

---

swell(-swelled-swollen)
　부풀다, 팽창하다
triumph 승리감, 쾌감
torment 고통을 주다, 고문하다

stir[stəːr] 움직이다, 선동하다
commit 저지르다
haunt …에 자주 가다
deformed 추한, 불구의

· ·

20 She, not I, would suffer for the murder I committed!
　내가 아니라, 그녀가 내가 저지른 살인으로 고통받게
　될 것이었다!
5 someone as deformed and horrible as myself
　could not deny herself to me
　그녀가 나만큼이나 기형이고
　끔찍한 존재라면 나를
　거부하지는 않을 것이다

괴물은 Frankenstein에게 무엇
을 요구하고 있는가?

① to create a female
　monster
② to kill him
③ to be his friend

ANS. ①

The monster finished speaking and stared at me expecting an answer. I was trying to understand exactly what he wanted me to do. The creature continued, "You must create a female for
5 me with whom I can live and exchange thoughts and ideas. I demand it. You must not refuse."

"I do indeed refuse," I replied; "and no torture could make me do it. Be gone!"

"You are in the wrong," the fiend replied. "I am
10 not threatening you, but I am trying to reason with you. I am malicious because I am miserable. I will seek revenge for my injuries. If I cannot inspire love, I will inspire fear—mostly against you! I will destroy you and you will regret the day you were born!"

As he spoke his face was twisted in a way that was too horrible for humans to look at. He calmed himself down and continued, "If anyone were kind to me, I would be a hundred times kinder to him. What I am asking for is reasonable and moderate. Of course, we will be monsters, but if you agree, neither you nor any other human shall ever see us again. We will go to the wilds of South America. I want to paint a picture of peace and contentment for you."

---

fiend[fi:nd] 악마(처럼 냉혹한 사람)
threaten 협박하다, 위협하다
malicious 악의가 있는

inspire (남에게 사상, 감정을)
일어나게 하다
contentment 만족

· ·

7 no torture could make me do it
어떤 고문을 가해도 난 그런 일은 할 수 없소
⌐ in a way that was too horrible for
humans to look at 인간이 바라보기에는
너무나 끔찍한 모습으로
7 neither you nor any other human
shall ever see us again
당신도 어떤 다른 사람도
우리를 다시는 보지
못할 거요

본문에 나타난 monster의 어조가
<u>아닌</u> 것은?

① persuasive

② threatening

③ exhausted

I was moved, but replied, "How can someone who craves the sympathy and company of men spend his life away from them? You will return and meet with their contempt. Then you will 5 resume your evil ways. I cannot agree to your request."

"I swear that I and my companion will forever leave the sight of mankind. And even when I am on my deathbed, I will not curse you, my creator."

10   His words had a strange effect on me. Although I could not sympathize with him, I felt it was not right to keep him from this happiness. "I will agree to your demand if you promise that you will leave Europe and every other place that humans live as 15 soon as I have made a female to go with you."

"I do swear," he cried. "Go home and start to work now. I will watch your work anxiously. And don't worry, as soon as you are ready, I will appear again."

20   As soon as he said this, he left. Maybe he was afraid that I would change my mind. I watched him descend the mountain with the speed of an

eagle. His story had taken the whole day to tell and, since it was getting dark, I headed home. The next morning, I set out for my father's home in Geneva.

move …의 마음을 움직이다
crave 열망하다, 갈망하다
sympathy 동정, 공감
company 친구,(사교적) 회합
contempt 경멸
resume [rizú:m] 다시 시작하다
swear(-swore-sworn) 맹세하다
deathbed 죽음의 자리, 임종
anxiously 마음 졸이며
descend 내려가다

1 How can someone who craves the sympathy and company of men spend their his away from them? 인간의 동정과 동반을 갈망하는 사람이 어떻게 인간과 떨어져 지낼 수 있겠는가?

11 I felt it was not right to keep him from this happiness 그에게서 이런 행복을 빼앗는 것은 옳지 않다고 느껴졌지요

1 His story had taken the whole day to tell 그의 이야기는 하루 종일 지속되었습니다

Quiz

Frankenstein이 여자 괴물을 만들어주는 조건으로, 괴물이 한 약속은 무엇인가?
우리말로 간단히 설명하시오.

ANS. 영원히 (유럽을 떠나) 인간의 눈에 띄지 않겠다

II
Comprehension Checkup

I. Justine이 William의 살인범으로 몰린 까닭이 <u>아닌</u> 것은?

① 살인이 일어난 장소 근처에서
   Justine을 목격한 사람이 있다.
② Justine에게서 William이
   갖고 있던 사진이 발견되었다.
③ Justine이 사건이 일어난
   시각에 William과 함께 있었다.

2. 괴물이 오두막에 사는 사람들에게 취한 행동이 <u>아닌</u> 것은?

① 그들에게 땔감을 마련해 주었다.
② 그들에게 식량을 구해다 주었다.
③ 그들을 관찰함으로써 그들의 언어를 배웠다.

3. 오두막에 사는 노인이 괴물에게
   친절할 수 있었던 까닭은?

① because he was blind
② because he needed some
   help from the monster
③ because he knew that the monster helped his family

4. 괴물이 오두막의 가족들에게 접근한
진정한 이유는 무엇인지 다음 빈 칸을 채우시오.

He approached and observed the family
because he needed some _____.

① food   ② friends
③ place to live in

5. 다음 ①~④를 사건이 일어난 순서대로 배열하시오.

① The monster killed William.
② Justine was accused of William's murder.
③ The monster spent the winter observing the family in
   the cottage.
④ The monster asked Frankenstein to make a female
   monster.

6. 다음 밑줄 친 단어와 바꾸어 쓸 수 있는 표현은?

I will slaughter everyone who crosses my path.

① murder   ② miss   ③ look after

7. 다음 중 괴물이 한 말이 아닌 것은?

① Your humanity assures me of success with those
   friends I shall soon meet.
② There was no person on earth who would pity or help me.
③ You will return and meet with their contempt.

Chapter 3

Weeks past at my father's house, I couldn't begin my work. I was not enthusiastic about creating another 5 monster, so I delayed it. The delay caused my health to improve in the relaxed atmosphere of the family home. My father noticed this. "I am happy to see, my dear son, that you have resumed your 10 former pleasures," he began, "but it troubles me that you still spend so much time alone. I confess, my son, that I have always wanted you and Elizabeth to marry. I know you may think of her as your sister and may not want her to be your 15 wife. I know it is also possible that you may love another woman."

"My dear father, reassure yourself that I love my cousin tenderly and dearly. My future hopes are entirely tied to expecting
5 our marriage."

"Victor," said my father, "your feelings bring me more joy than I could possibly know. Please tell me that you will agree to an immediate marriage to her."

---

enthusiastic [enθuːziǽstik]
　　　　열심인, 열광적인
improve 좋게 하다, 향상시키다

relaxed 긴장을 푼, 편한
atmosphere 분위기
immediate 즉시의

· ·

7 The delay caused my health to improve
(여자 괴물 만드는 일의) 지연은 나의 건강을 회복시켜 주었어요
9 I'm happy to see that you have resumed your former pleasures 네가 다시 예전의 기쁨을 회복한 걸 보아서 기쁘구나
3 My future hopes are entirely tied to expecting our marriage.
미래의 제 희망은 전적으로 우리 결혼에 대한 기대에 달려 있습니다.

What Frankenstein's father wants is _____ .

① his success in study
② his marriage to Elizabeth
③ his staying at home

ANS. ②

71

The idea of marrying Elizabeth right away was one of horror and dismay. I had promised to make another creature. If I broke that promise, who knows what horrors the monster may bring to my 5 family? I told my father that I needed to go to England before marrying. But I did not tell him the real reason for my visit was to complete my promise to the monster.

My father agreed and let me decide how long I 10 would be away and I agreed to marry Elizabeth immediately upon my return. My father and Elizabeth agreed to have Clerval to accompany me to England. Henry would interrupt my solitude,

but it was good to have so close a friend with me. Henry might even prevent my enemy from interfering with my work.

We left for England in September. We visited many places of learning and talked with many scholars. Henry found that a traveler's life can be a difficult one.

---

dismay 실망
creature 피조물, 생물
complete 완성하다
immediately 즉시

accompany 동반하다, 따라가다
interrupt[ìntərʌ́pt] 가로막다
solitude 고독, 외로움
interfere 방해하다

· ·

11 upon my return 내가 돌아오자마자
13 Henry would interrupt my solitude
헨리가 나를 외롭지 않게 해줄 것이었죠
2 Henry might even prevent my enemy from
interfering with my work. 헨리는 적이 내 작업을
방해하는 것을 막아 주기까지 할지도 모릅니다.

The reason why
Frankenstein wants to go to
England before marriage is
to complete the _____ to
the _____.

ANS. promise, monster

Scotland was not much his liking although he always made the best of every situation. We had been away for some time so I proposed to go there alone. "Leave me alone for a month or two. When we meet again, I hope my mood will be better and 5 I will be a better companion for you."

"I'd rather be with you in your solitude than with these Scots whom I don't know. But hurry, my friend, and return so that I can at least feel somewhat at home." 10

When we parted I traveled to the remotest part of the Orkneys to continue my labors. The island

 was virtually unin habited and I could work at 15 my horrid task uninterrupted. I worked in the mornings, but when the 20 weather per- mitted, I went

for long walks in the evenings. Every day became more horrible than the last. Sometimes I couldn't go to the laboratory at all. Sometimes I worked day and night without stopping. At every moment
5 I was afraid that I was going to meet my persecutor. The work made me sick, but I knew I had to continue.

propose 제안하다
remote 외딴, 멀리 떨어진
virtually 사실상, 실질적으로
uninhabited 사람이 살지 않는

horrid 지긋지긋하게 싫은, 무서운
uninterrupted 중단되지 않은
persecutor[pə́ːrsikjùːtər]
　　　　박해자, 학대자

....

1 Scotland was not much his liking
그는 스코틀랜드를 그다지 좋아하지 않았어요
7 I'd rather be with you in your solitude than with these Scots whom I don't know. 나는 생판 모르는 스코틀랜드
사람들과 함께 있느니 고독해하는 자네와 함께 있고 싶군.
9 so that I can at least feel somewhat at home
내가 조금이나마 편안함을 느낄 수 있도록
14 I could work at my horrid task
uninterrupted 나는 방해받지
않은 채 내 끔찍한 과업을
수행할 수 있었습니다

Frankenstein이 친구와 헤어져
외딴 곳으로 간 이유를 우리말로
간단히 설명하시오.

One evening late at night I sat in my laboratory and thought back to three years earlier[5] when I had been in the same situation. Even though the fiend I created may promised to stay away from people, she may not. If she[10] were a thinking being, she might refuse to agree to a promise made before her creation. Or perhaps they would hate each other. Even if they left Europe, the demon would probably want her to have children. Did I have the right to force this[15] situation on the rest of humanity?

I trembled and felt sick inside when I looked up and there, by the moonlight stood the demon I had created. Yes, it had followed me on my travels and now he had come to check on my progress[20] and claim his promise. As I looked on him, I thought I must have been mad to agree to such a promise. Trembling with passion, I tore apart the new creature I was creating. The wretch saw me

5 and with a howl of despair and revenge, he slipped away.

laboratory 실험실
tremble 떨다
progress 경과, (일이) 되어감

howl[haul] 울부짖음
despair 절망, 자포자기
revenge 복수

. . . .

3 (I) thought back to three years earlier when I had been in the same situation 내가 동일한 상황에 있었던 3년 전을 회상해 보았어요

15 Did I have the right to force this situation on the rest of humanity? 인류를 이러한 궁지로 몰아넣을 권리가 나에게 있는가?

22 I must have been mad to agree to such a promise
내가 그러한 약속에 동의하다니 제정신이
아니었음에 틀림없습니다

1 Trembling with passion
격정으로 몸을 부르르 떨면서

What did Frankenstein do with the new creature?

① He finally gave life to her.

② He tore it apart.

③ He gave her to the monster.

ANS. ②

I stood for several hours gazing out the window. Then I heard footsteps in the hallway. The door opened and the dreadful wretch appeared. He approached me and said, "You have 5 destroyed the work you began. What do you intend to do? Do you dare break your promise? I left Switzerland with you and endured unbelievable cold, hunger and fatigue as I followed you. Do you dare to destroy my hopes?"

10 "Be gone! I am breaking my promise. I will never create another like you!"

"Slave, I reasoned with you before, but you have proven untrustworthy. Remember I have power. I can make you so miserable that you will 15 hate to see the daylight. You are my creator, but I am your master. Obey!"

"Be gone! I have made up my mind and your words will only make me angrier!"

The monster saw how determined I was. He 20 was filled with rage. "Am I the only being who will be denied a spouse? You may hate me, but watch out! Your life will pass in total misery. You can criticize my other passions, but I still want revenge. You will be sorry for causing me pain!"

gaze 응시하다
footstep 발자국
hallway 복도
dreadful 무시무시한
wretch 비열한 사람
destroy 파괴하다
endure 인내하다, 참다
unbelievable 믿을 수 없는
fatigue [fətíːg] 피로
reason 설득하다
untrustworthy 신뢰할 수 없는
spouse 배우자
criticize 비난하다

9 Do you dare to destroy my hopes?
감히 나의 희망을 파괴해 버리다니?

12 you have proven untrustworthy
약속을 지키지 않았다

20 Am I the only being who will
be denied a spouse?
나는 배우자를 맞지 못하는
유일한 존재가 아닌가?

Frankenstein decided not to _____.

① create another monster
② marry Elizabeth
③ go back home

ANS. 1

"Stop, you devil! I am not afraid of you. Leave me."

"All right, I'll go. But remember I will be with you on your wedding night."

5 I started towards him and exclaimed, "Before you threaten me, make sure you are safe!"

I would have grabbed him but he quickly left the house. In a few minutes he was in his boat racing across the waters at superhuman speed.
10 Soon he was out of sight.

Everything was quiet again, but his words rang in my ears. Why didn't I follow him and kill him on the spot? But I let him get away and he was headed toward the mainland. I was shattered at
15 the thought of who his next victim might be. And then again I thought of his words, "I will be with you on your wedding night." I thought of my poor Elizabeth and how sad she would be to lose her lover in such a tragic way. I made up my mind not
20 to die without a struggle.

After a restless night I decided to rejoin Clerval and then return to Geneva. I put the remains of the female monster into a basket. At about 3:00 in the morning I climbed into my boat and sailed for the mainland. About 4 miles from shore; I sank the basket to the bottom of the sea.

start (놀람 · 공포로) 움찔하다	victim 희생자, 피해자
exclaim 소리치다	tragic 비극적인
threaten 협박하다	struggle [strʌ́gəl] 투쟁, 분투
grab 움켜잡다, 움켜쥐다	restless 불안한
shatter …의 감정을	rejoin 재회하다
강렬하게 뒤흔들다	remains 잔존물, 잔해, 유해

• •

3 I will be with you on your wedding night.
당신의 결혼식 날 밤에 오겠다.

11 his words rang in my ears 그의 말이 내 귓가에서 맴돌았습니다

18 how sad she would be to lose her lover in such a tragic way
사랑하는 사람을 그렇게 비극적으로 잃게 된다면 그녀가 얼마나 애통할 것인지

19 I made up my mind not to die without a struggle.
나는 싸워 보지도 않고 죽지는 않으리라 결심했지요.

'his words rang in my ears' 에서 밑줄 친 부분이 의미하는 것 을 본문에서 찾아 쓰시오.

ANS. I will be with you on your wedding night.

After a very frightening voyage in a very rough and windy sea, I arrived at a place with a wild rocky border. I got out of the 5 boat and spoke the first strangers I saw. "My good friends," I began, "will you be so kind as to tell me where I 10 am?"

"You'll know soon enough," he replied gruffly.

"Why do you answer me so roughly?" I replied. "Are Englishmen always so rude to strangers?"

"I'm not English," said the man. "This is Ireland 15 and it is an Irish custom to hate villains. You must come now directly to see Mr. Kirwin, the magistrate."

I was soon taken to Mr. Kirwin who was a kind old gentleman with good manners. But he looked 20 at me quite severely as he called forward witnesses. Apparently, the night before a stranger had been murdered in the village. The stranger was a handsome man about 25 years old. He seemed to have been strangled because there were the black marks of fingers around his neck.

frightening 무서운, 굉장한	villain 악인, 악한
voyage 항해	magistrate [mǽdʒəstrèit]
rough 거친, 험한	치안 판사, 행정 장관
rocky 암석이 많은	manners 예의, 예절
border 경계, 국경	severely 호되게, 격심하게
stranger 이방인	witness 증인, 증언
gruffly 퉁명스럽게	apparently 명백히, 외견상으로는
custom 관습	strangle 교살하다, 질식사시키다

· ·

9 will you be so kind as to tell me where I am?
   여기가 어디인지 말씀 좀 해주시겠어요?

21 as he called forward witnesses
   그가 목격자들을 앞으로 소환했을 때

2 He seemed to have been strangled
   그는 교살당한 것 같았습니다

Frankenstein은 왜 치안 판사에게 불려갔는가?

① 외국인 입국시 관례상
② 살인범으로 의심받아서
③ 피해자의 신원을 확인하고자

ANS. 2

When the finger marks were mentioned, I thought immediately of my brother and became quite upset. The magistrate noticed this quite obviously and read it as a sign of my guilt.

5   A woman said that about an hour before she heard of the murder she saw a man alone in a boat leave from near where the body was found. Several other witnesses confirmed this account. The strangers I had first met confirmed that I had

10 landed near the murder spot and that I had probably been unable to escape because of the rough weather the night before.

On hearing the evidence, Mr. Kirwin had me taken to view the body. I was taken to the room

where the body lay and led up to the coffin. How can I describe my feelings when I saw the corpse? The body was Henry Clerval! I gasped for breath and throwing myself on his lifeless body. I exclaimed, "Have my murderous deeds also killed you, my dearest Henry? I have already killed two people and now other victims are waiting for their destiny. But you, Clerval, my friend..."

mention 언급하다	coffin 관
obviously 명백하게	describe 묘사하다
confirm 확인하다	corpse[kɔːrps] 시신
account 설명	gasp 헐떡거리다, 숨이 차다
evidence 증거	murderous 살인의, 흉악한

13 On hearing the evidence 그 증언을 듣고 나자
14 I was taken to the room where the body lay
   나는 시체가 안치된 방으로 안내되었습니다
4 throwing myself on his lifeless body
   그의 시체 위에 엎드려서

Who was murdered?
Answer in English.

ANS. [Frankenstein's friend, Henry Clerval]

I could no longer stand and was carried out of the room in convulsions. A fever struck me and I lay ill for two months. During my illness, I accused myself of the murderer of William, Justine and Clerval.

Why didn't I die? I was doomed to live and after two months I found myself feeling as if I were waking from a dream. I was in a prison surrounded by guards and bars and all the other horrible things of a prison.

One day as I was recovering, Mr. Kirwin came to see me. He said that he knew that he would be little comfort to me. My best friend was dead and I was accused of his murder. It was almost like some evil fiend had planned it that way. Seeing the surprise in

my face he continued, "As soon as you became sick, I went through your papers to discover if you had any relatives to whom I could write and explain your situation. I found a letter from your
5 father and immediately wrote to him. It has been two months since I wrote, but I am worried that you may not be able to withstand any excitement."

---

convulsion [kənvʌ́lʃən] 경련   recover 회복하다
doom …의 운명을 정하다   relative 친척, 친족
surround 둘러싸다   withstand 잘 견디다, …에 저항하다

· ·

7 as if I were waking from a dream
마치 꿈속에서 깨어난 것처럼
20 It was almost like some evil fiend had planned it that
way. 그것은 마치 사악한 악마가 그런 식으로 음모를
꾸민 것 같았지요.
2 if you had any relatives to whom I could
write and explain your situation
내가 편지를 써서 당신의 상황을
얘기해 줄 친척이 있는지

Where is Frankenstein now?

① in a prison
② in a hospital
③ at home

ANS. 😊

"The suspense is much worse! Please tell me now whose death I now have to cry over."

"Your family is perfectly well," said the magistrate, "and someone, a friend has come to visit you. It is your father."

I was delighted. As he entered the room, I asked, "Are you safe—and Elizabeth—and Ernest?" My father assured me that everyone was all right. He felt so sorry for me. He thought that I had traveled to find happiness but some fatality seemed to be following me. I heartily agreed with him. "Yes, my father, some doom hangs over me and I must live to fulfill it. Otherwise I would have died on poor Henry's coffin."

We weren't allowed to talk for too long since my health was still not good. We met several times, however, before the date of my trial. At my trial, the kind Mr. Kirwin made sure that I had a good defense and it was soon proven that I had still been in the Orkneys at the time of Henry's murder.

As soon as possible after my release, my father

and I set sail for Geneva. I was extremely anxious to get there and destroy the monster I had created.

---

suspense 걱정, 불안
perfectly 완전히, 완벽하게
delighted 기쁜
assure (확신시켜) 안심하게 하다
fatality[feitǽləti] 불행
heartily 매우, 진심으로
doom 불운, 죽음

fulfill 성취하다, 완성하다
otherwise 만약 그렇지 않으면
trial 재판
defense 변호, (피고의) 항변
release 석방
extremely 극도로, 몹시
anxious 매우 …하고 싶어하는

. . . .

1 Please tell me now whose death I now have to cry over.
이제 누구의 죽음을 슬퍼해야 하는지 말해 주십시오.

10 some fatality seemed to be following me
어떤 불운이 나를 따라다니는 것 같습니다

12 some doom hangs over me
어떤 (피할 수 없는) 운명이 나에게 다가옵니다

13 Otherwise I would have died on poor Henry's coffin.
그렇지 않았더라면 헨리의 관 앞에서 죽었을 겁니다.

Who came to visit
Frankenstein?

① his father
② Elizabeth
③ Ernest

ANS. 1

In Paris, I found my health was not good enough to continue to travel, so we stayed there. During that time I refused to go out in public and often accused myself of the murder of William,
5 Justine and Henry. My father begged me to stop and surely thought that I was quite mad.

Shortly before we left Paris a letter came from Elizabeth. She was greatly concerned about my health and asked if I was so miserable because I
10 was about to marry her. She assured me of her love but wondered if I loved another. She also assured me if that were the case, I was free since she desired only my happiness.

Her letter brought back to me what I had
15 forgotten, the threat of the fiend–"I will be with you on your wedding night." Poor sweet Elizabeth! I read her letter repeatedly. I would die to make her happy. If the monster executed his threat, death was inevitable. I thought whether marriage
20 would actually hasten my fate.

public 공중의, 공개의
concerned 걱정하는
desire 바라다, 갈망하다
threat 위협
repeatedly 반복해서
execute 실행하다
inevitable [inévitəvəl]
　　불가피한, 피할 수 없는
actually 실제로는
hasten 재촉하다, 서두르다

---

8 She was greatly concerned about my health
　그녀는 나의 건강에 대해 상당히 걱정을 하고 있었어요
10 She assured me of her love
　그녀는 나에게 그녀의 사랑을 확신시켰지요
12 since she desired only my happiness
　그녀는 단지 나의 행복만을 바랬기 때문에
14 Her letter brought back to me what I had
　forgotten 그녀의 편지는 내가
　잊고 있었던 것을 상기시켰습니다

빈 칸에 알맞은 말을 본문에서
찾아 쓰시오.

Why did they stay in Paris
on the way to Geneva?

Because _____.

ANS. Frankenstein's health was not good
enough to continue to travel

He had vowed to be with me on my wedding night. Didn't he understand that the threat meant he wouldn't kill me until then? I vowed that if my marriage would bring about happiness to my
5 father and Elizabeth, my enemy's threats would not delay that a single hour.

In this state of mind I wrote to Elizabeth, calmly and affectionately. "Don't worry, my dear girl. It is you alone that I love. But I have one
10 secret, Elizabeth, and it is a dreadful one. When I tell you, you will be horrified. I will tell you this secret the day after our marriage. But
15 until then, I beg you not to speak to anyone about it. I must have your absolute confidence in this. I know you will
20 agree."

About a week after her letter arrived, we arrived

in Geneva and Elizabeth met us. Shortly after our arrival, my father spoke to me about marriage to Elizabeth. "Do you have another
5 woman?" he asked.

I assured him that it was Elizabeth alone that I loved and that I would dedicate myself in life and in death to her happiness.

vow 맹세하다, 서약하다
delay 지연시키다
affectionately 애정이 넘치게

absolute[ǽbsəlùːt] 확실한
confidence 신뢰, 확신
dedicate 바치다

5 my enemy's threats would not delay that a single hour
내 적의 위협이 그것을 조금이라도 지연시키도록 내버려두지 않을 것입니다

9 It is you alone that I love.
내가 사랑하는 사람은 당신뿐입니다.

17 I must have your absolute confidence in this. 당신은 이 점에 있어서 절대로 신뢰를 지켜야 합니다.

7 I would dedicate myself in life and in death to her happiness.
나는 살든지 죽든지 그녀의 행복을 위해 헌신하겠습니다.

'my enemy's threats would not delay that a single hour'에서 밑줄 친 것이 무엇을 가리키는지 본문에서 찾아 쓰시오.

ANS. happiness to my father and Elizabeth

My father urged me not to talk that way and encouraged me that soon after we married, we should have children. That would replace those lives that had been so cruelly taken away from us. We then agreed that the wedding would take place in ten days. That, I imagined, would seal my fate.

My god! If I had for an instant considered what the monster had in store for me I would have left forever from my native land and wandered friendless over the earth. I was prepared for my own death, but I only hastened the death of a far dearer victim.

As the wedding date approached, I took every precaution in case the monster should try to attack me in the open. I carried knives and handguns. Elizabeth seemed happy, and my calm state of mind seemed to assure her. On the day of the wedding, however, she was a little sad as she thought of the secret I was to reveal to her.

After the ceremony we set sail across Lake Geneva on our honeymoon. I was delighted, but those were the last days I was ever to be happy.

urge 강력히 권고하다	precaution [prikɔ́ːʃən] 조심, 경계
replace …에 대신하다	state 상태
cruelly 잔인하게	reveal 알려주다, 누설하다
seal 밀봉하다, 막다	ceremony 예식
approach 다가오다	honeymoon 신혼여행

· ·

3 That would replace those lives that had been so cruelly
taken away from us. 그것은 우리에게서 너무나 잔인하게 취해진 그
생명들을 대신해 줄 것이었습니다.

5 that the wedding would take place in ten days
열흘 후에 결혼식이 있을 것이라고

14 in case the monster should try to attack me in the open
야외에서 그 괴물이 나를 공격할 경우를 대비해

18 as she thought of the secret I was to reveal to her
내가 그녀에게 말해 주기로 한 그 비밀을 생각할 때

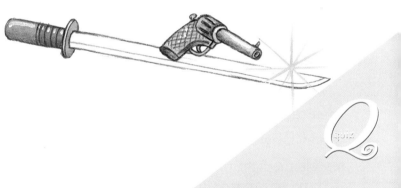

'those were the last days I
was ever to be happy'는
무엇을 암시하는가?

① Elizabeth의 죽음
② 괴물과의 격투
③ 자신의 죽음

ANS. ①

We landed at 8 o'clock. We walked for a little while on the shore and then went to our rooms at the inn. I had been calm during the day, but as it began to grow dark, I became anxious and fearful. My hand held onto the gun in my pocket, and every sound terrified me. I vowed that I would not die without a fight until either my life or the life of my enemy was extinguished.

Elizabeth silently watched my agitation for some time. I told her that after this night all would be well. Suddenly I thought about how terrible the fight that I soon expected would be for my wife. I urged her to go to bed and decided not to join her until I had some knowledge about the situation regarding my enemy.

She left me and I continued to walk up and

down the hallways of the inn. I saw no sight of him. Suddenly my wanderings were interrupted by a dreadful scream. It came from the room where Elizabeth had gone. The whole truth rushed into my head and my arms dropped to my side. This state only lasted an instant as I heard another scream and ran into the room.

anxious 불안한, 걱정스런   regarding …에 관하여
extinguish 잃게 하다, 절멸시키다   wandering 산책, 방랑
agitation[ædʒətéiʃən] 동요   scream 비명
....

13 until either my life or the life of my enemy was extinguished
나의 생명이나 내 적의 생명 중 하나가 소멸될 때까지는

20 until I had some knowledge about the situation
regarding my enemy 내 적의 정황을 파악할 때까지는

1 I saw no sight of him. 그는 내 시야에 나타나지 않았습니다.

2 my wanderings were interrupted by a
dreadful scream 끔찍한 비명소리를
듣고 나는 걸음을 멈추었어요

본문의 배경에 대한 설명으로 적절
치 않은 것은?

① 신혼여행 중이다.
② 긴장감이 감돈다.
③ 아주 이른 새벽이다.

ANS. 3

Good God! Why didn't I die there on the spot?
Why am I still alive to tell about the death of the
best and purest person on the earth? She was
there, lifeless and unmoving, thrown across the
5 bed with her head hanging over the edge. Could I
look at this and live? Alas! Life is stubborn and
clings closest where it is most hated. I fell
senseless to the ground.

When I recovered I found myself surrounded by
10 people of the inn. I rushed from them into the
room where the body of Elizabeth lay. I embraced
her with passion, but her cold body told me that
this was no longer the Elizabeth I had loved and

cherished. The murderous mark of the fiend was on her neck and breath had stopped flowing from her lips.

While I still held her, I happened to look up. The window shutters were open and there stood the face of that horrible and hated monster. A grin was on his evil face and he seemed to jeer as a fiendish figure pointed to the corpse of my wife. I rushed to the window, pulled out my gun and fired, but he escaped and running with the speed of lightening, dove into the lake.

---

stubborn[stʌ́bərn] 완고한, 다루기 어려운
embrace 포옹하다, 껴안다
cherish 소중히 하다

horrible 무서운, 끔찍한
grin (이를 드러내고) 싱긋이 웃다
jeer 조롱하다, 비웃다
fiendish 악마 같은, 극악한

· ·

5 with her head hanging over the edge
그녀의 머리가 침대 가장자리에 재껴진 채

7 I fell senseless to the ground.
나는 기절해 바닥에 쓰러졌지요.

4 I happened to look up
나는 우연히 위를
올려다보았습니다

What happened to
Elizabeth?

① She was murdered.
② She fainted.
③ She died of a heart
attack.

ANS. 1

The death of William, the execution of Justine, the murder of Clerval and lastly my wife; even at that moment I didn't know if my remaining friends were safe from the monster. My father
5 might at this moment be struggling with the fiend, while Ernest lay dead at his feet.

I decided to go back to Geneva, but since I could not get a horse or a boat at that time of night, my trip was delayed until morning. My
10 father and Ernest were alive, but my father collapsed when he heard the news I brought. He could not live under the horrors that were surrounding him. He was unable to get out of his bed and a few days later, he died in my arms.

15 I lost sensation and slipped into melancholy. As the memory of past misfortunes pressed on me, I began to think about their cause–the monster I had created and then sent out into the world for my destruction. I was insanely angry when I
20 thought of him and prayed that I might catch him so that I could smash in his cursed head.

I didn't want my hate to be useless, so I went

to a local magistrate and told him the entire story. While he was sympathetic, he was not at all encouraging that the monster could be captured. I left his house in an angry mood and retired to ⁵think of some other way to exact my revenge.

execution 처형	insanely 미친 듯이
collapse[kəlǽps] 맥없이 쓰러지다, 실신하다	sympathetic 동정적인
	encouraging 격려하는, 장려하는
sensation 감각, 감정	capture 붙잡다
melancholy 우울, 침울	retire 물러가다, 후퇴하다
destruction 파괴	exact 싫건 좋건 …하다, 강요하다

• •

4 My father might at this moment be struggling with the fiend, while Ernest lay dead at his feet.
지금 이 순간, 아버지는 그 악마와 싸우고 있고, 그의 발 아래 어니스트가 쓰러져 죽어 있을지도 모릅니다.

15 As the memory of past misfortunes pressed on me
과거 불행한 기억이 밀려오자

21 so that I could smash in his cursed head
그의 저주스러운 머리를 뭉개버리기 위해

2 he was not at all encouraging
그는 전혀 용기를 북돋아
주지 않았습니다

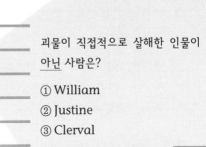

괴물이 직접적으로 살해한 인물이
아닌 사람은?

① William
② Justine
③ Clerval

ANS. 2

1

Comprehension Checkup

I. Frankenstein이 Elizabeth와 결혼하는 것을 주저한 까닭은?

① because he didn't love her any more

② because he was afraid of the horrors the monster may bring to his family

③ because he wanted to be a great scienti:
before marriage

2. 밑줄 친 부분이 공통적으로 지칭하는 것은?

● <u>The work</u> made me sick, but I knew I had to continue.

● I must have been mad to agree to <u>such a promise</u>.

① to take care of the monster

② to create a female monster

③ to be a great scientist

3. 다음 밑줄 친 'This'가 공통으로 가리키는 것은 무엇인지
영어로 쓰시오.

● <u>This</u> was created by Frankenstein.

● <u>This</u> murdered many people.

● <u>This</u> felt so lonely on earth and wanted some friends.

4. Frankenstein이 여자 괴물 만드는 일을 포기한
궁극적인 이유는?

① 또 다른 괴물이 인간에게 끼칠 공포를 생각해서
② 괴물이 약속을 지키지 않을 것이 두려워서
③ 괴물의 행복을 바라지 않아서

5. 다음에 나열된 인물들의 공통점은?

William, Justine, Elizabeth, Henry

→ They are all _____ of the monster.

① victims   ② murderers   ③ accusers

6. 지명과 그 장소에 대한 설명으로 바르지 <u>않은</u> 것은?

① Geneva - Frankenstein의 가족이 사는 곳
② Paris - 여자 괴물을 만들던 곳
③ Ireland - Clerval이 살해된 곳

7. Elizabeth의 죽음이 직접적으로
야기한 것은?

① Ernest의 죽음
② Frankenstein의 아버지의 죽음
③ 괴물을 죽이기 위한 치안판사의 즉각적인 협조

정답은 p.129에

Chapter 4

My first decision was to leave Geneva forever. My country, which when I was happy was so dear to me, was now hateful to me. I gathered some money and began the wanderings that will only end with death.

5

The night before I was to leave I visited the cemetery where William, Elizabeth and my father were buried. Everything was silent. The deep grief that I felt soon gave way to rage and despair. I vowed then and there by the earth on which I knelt to pursue the demon that caused all this misery until either he or I die in deadly battle. I felt the presence of spirits and I prayed to them; "Let the cursed and hellish monster drink deep of agony; let him feel the deep despair that now torments me." I was answered through the stillness of night by a loud and fiendish laugh.

9 The deep grief that I felt soon gave way to rage and despair.
내가 느꼈던 깊은 슬픔은 곧 분노와 절망으로 바뀌었어요.
3 Let the cursed and hellish monster drink deep of agony.
저주받은 사악한 괴물이 깊은 고통의 잔을 마시게 하소서.
5 I was answered through the stillness of night by a loud and fiendish laugh. 고요한 밤의 적막을 뚫고 요란스럽고 사악한 웃음소리가 들려왔습니다.

제네바를 떠나기 전에
Frankenstein이 들른 곳은
어디인지 우리말로 쓰시오.

5

It rang loud and long in my ears and I felt as if hell was surrounding me in mockery and laughter. The laughter died away, when a well-known and hated voice, 5 apparently close to my ear, addressed me in a loud whisper, "I am satisfied, you miserable wretch! You have decided to live and I am satisfied."

I ran toward the spot where the sound came 10 from, but the devil escaped me. Suddenly the moon arose and shone full upon his horrid shape as he ran with superhuman speed. I followed him and for many months this has been my task. I followed the Rhone River in vain. The blue 15 Mediterranean appeared and by a strange chance I saw the fiend enter a ship headed for the Black Sea. I took passage on the same ship, but I don't know how the monster escaped.

In the wilds of Russia he evaded me. 20 Sometimes the peasants, scared by his horrid appearance told me where he was headed. Since he was afraid that if I lost all trace of him, I would

despair and die, he
sometimes left some
mark for me to follow.
I endured cold, want
5 and fatigue. I was
cursed by some
devil and carried
with me my own personal hell.

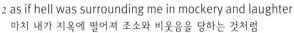

mockery 조롱, 비웃음   peasant [pézənt] 농부
address …에게 말을 걸다   appearance 외관, 모양
horrid 무서운   endure 참다, 인내하다
evade 피하다   curse 저주하다
. . . .

2 as if hell was surrounding me in mockery and laughter
  마치 내가 지옥에 떨어져 조소와 비웃음을 당하는 것처럼

20 the peasants, scared by his horrid appearance told
  me where he was headed 그 (괴물)의 흉칙한 모습에
  놀란 농부들이 그가 어디로 향해 갔는지 내게
  말해 줬습니다

21 Since he was afraid that if I lost all
  trace of him, I would despair
  and die 괴물은 내가
  그의 발자취를 완전히
  놓쳐 절망에 빠져
  죽을까 봐

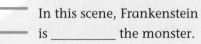

In this scene, Frankenstein
is _____ the monster.

① avoiding
② fighting with
③ chasing

ANS. 3

Sometimes when I was on the point of starvation a feast was provided for me–I believed by those spirits to whom I had prayed. When I could, I followed rivers, but the monster usually
5 avoided these since that was where the most people were. In more barren places, I lived by eating wild animals I trapped. I had money and gained the friendship of villagers by passing it out. My life and how it passed were indeed hateful to me.

10   I had no idea what the monster's feelings were. Sometimes he left messages for me on the trunks of trees, or carved in stone that guided me and enraged me. "My reign is not over. You live and my power is complete. Follow me. I am going to
15 the North Pole where you will feel the misery of the cold that I won't. You will find a dead rabbit near here. Eat it and feel refreshed. Come my enemy, we have yet to wrestle for our lives."

Another inscription read, "Prepare! Your work is
20 just beginning. Wrap yourself up in furs and get some food. We shall soon enter a journey where your sufferings will satisfy my everlasting hatred."

starvation 굶주림
feast 진수성찬
provide 제공하다
spirit 정령, 요정
barren (땅이) 메마른
enrage[enréidʒ] 격분시키다
reign 세력, 지배
inscription 비문, 명각
everlasting 영원히 계속되는

. . . .

1 when I was on the point of starvation
내가 굶어 죽으려고 하는 순간에

2 I believed by those spirits to whom I had prayed
나는 (진수성찬이) 내가 기도했던 정령에 의해 차려진 것이라고 믿었어요

13 My reign is not over. 내 힘은 아직 쇠하지 않았다.

15 where you will feel the misery of the cold that I won't
내가 느끼지 못하는 추위로 인해 네가
비참함을 느끼게 될 곳인

18 we have yet to wrestle for our lives
우리는 아직 생명을 걸고 겨뤄 보지 않았다
(이제부터 겨뤄 볼 참이다)

19 Another inscription read
또 다른 비문은 다음과
같이 씌어 있었습니다

괴물이 남긴 메시지가 <u>아닌</u> 것은?

① 나를 따라오는 것을 포기하라.
② 내 힘은 아직 쇠하지 않았다.
③ 나는 북극으로 갈 것이다.

I secured a sled and a dog team and found that I could actually gain on the monster. I stopped at a village to see if they had any information on him. The villagers told me that the night before a 5 huge monster had entered their village and taken a huge supply of food and a sled. I too secured supplies and continued my pursuit in earnest.

How much time has passed since then, I can only guess. I raced across the frozen sea on my 10 sled. I would think it was about three weeks after I left the village when I caught sight of him at last. He was no more than a mile ahead of me when I again lost him more utterly than ever before. The sea broke the ice between us and I was

stranded on an ice floe with my enemy racing off in the distance. Trapped on the floe, several of my dogs died and I thought I would die too.

I was about to sink in my despair when I saw your ship. I had no idea that ships ever came this far north. I destroyed part of my sled to make oars and rowed with great difficulty toward it.

secure [sikjúər] 확보하다
pursuit 추적
earnest 진지함, 진심

strand (배를) 좌초시키다
floe (해상에 떠있는) 빙원
distance (원)거리, 먼 곳

. . . .

12 He was no more than a mile ahead of me when I again lost him more utterly than ever before. 내가 그를 다시 완전히 놓쳤다고 생각했을 때, 그는 단지 나보다 1마일 앞선 곳에 있었습니다.

1 with my enemy racing off in the distance
내 적이 멀리서 질주하고 있었을 때

1

If you were heading south, I was determined to trust my fate to the sea rather than abandon my chase. I hoped to persuade you to give me a boat so I could pursue the monster. But you were headed north.

Oh! When will my guiding spirits allow me some rest? Must I die while he live? If that happens, Walton, swear to me that he will not escape and you will seek him to satisfy my vengeance in his death. When I am dead, if he should appear do not let him survive to add to his crimes. He is eloquent and persuasive, but don't

listen to him. His soul is as hellish as his body and full of treachery and fiend like evil. Don't listen to him. Call out the names of William, Justine, Clerval, Elizabeth, my father and ram your sword into his heart.

---

determine 결심하다, 결정하다   eloquent 말 잘하는, 웅변의
abandon 포기하다, 버리다   persuasive 설득력이 있는
persuade 설득하다   treachery 배신, 반역
vengeance[véndʒəns] 복수   ram 쑤셔 넣다

· ·

1 I was determined to trust my fate to the sea rather than abandon my chase 나는 추적을 포기하느니 차라리 바다에 내 운명을 맡기기로 결심했습니다
9 (swear to me that) you will seek him to satisfy my vengeance in his death 그를 찾아 죽임으로써 내 복수를 해 줄 것을 나에게 맹세해 주십시오
11 do not let him survive to add to his crimes 추가적인 범죄를 저지르도록 그를 살려 두어서는 안 됩니다

본문의 내용과 일치하지 <u>않는</u> 것은?

① Frankenstein은 우연히 Walton의 배를 만났다.
② Walton의 배는 북극을 향해 가고 있었다.
③ Walton도 그 괴물을 만나 얘기해 본 적이 있다.

ANS. ③

Walton continues.

August 26th, 17-

You have read this strange and terrific story, Margaret, and doesn't it curdle your blood like it 5 curdles mine? I cannot doubt that such a monster exists. I tried to learn from Frankenstein how he made it, but he absolutely refused to tell me.

"Are you mad, my friend?" he said. "Or do you want to let your own demon loose on the earth? 10 Learn my miseries and don't increase your own."

A week has past since he began the tale. We don't always talk about his misfortunes. He knows everything about literature. He must have been an even more wonderful man when he was not so miserable. Must I lose this wonderful person? I have longed for a friend who would sympathize with me and love me. Here, on the northern seas 5 I have found one. I worry, though that I will soon lose him. I want him to have hope in life and friendship, but he refuses.

"Thank you, Walton," he said, "but I must pursue and destroy the monster. Then my life on 0 earth will be fulfilled and I can die."

---

terrific 무서운, 지독한   absolutely 절대적으로
curdle [kə́:rdl] 응결시키다   loose 자유롭게 하다, 풀어주다

· ·

8 do you want to let your own demon loose on the earth?
당신이 만들어 낸 괴물이 지구를 맘껏 떠돌아다니게
하고 싶나요?

13 He must have been an even more
wonderful man 그는 훨씬 더 훌륭한 사람
이었음에 틀림없다

2 I have longed for a friend
나는 친구를 갈망해 왔단다

본문의 내용과 일치하면 T, 일치하지
않으면 F를 쓰시오.
( ) Walton believed in the
      existence of the monster.
( ) Frankenstein abandoned
      pursuing the monster.

ANS. T, F

5

September 2nd

My beloved sister,

I write to you surrounded by danger and I don't know if I will ever see England again. There are
5 mountains of ice all around us and I worry that we will be crushed. My brave crew's lives are in danger all due to my mad schemes.

My unfortunate guest tries to encourage me, and talks as if life were something he valued. Even
10 the crew is encouraged when he speaks. Even so I almost fear a mutiny.

---

crush 충돌하다
scheme 계획
mutiny[mjúːtəni] 폭동, 반란
demand 요청하다, 요구하다

request 요청, 요구
moderate 온화한, 적절한
present 현재의
hardship 역경

· ·

7 all due to my mad schemes 전적으로 나의 무모한 계획 때문에
9 who appeared not to have enough strength to speak
  말할 기운도 충분치 않아 보이는
10 His voice was so persuasive and moderate that the men
  were moved 그의 목소리는 너무나 설득력이 있고 온화해서 선원들은
  감동을 받았지
13 he collapsed, almost dying on the spot
  그는 쓰러졌고, 거의 그 자리에서 죽을 것 같았어

September 5th

We are still surrounded by ice and in danger of being crushed. Frankenstein's health gets worse each day. I mentioned in my last letter that I was
5 afraid of a mutiny. Today, several crewmembers came to my cabin and demanded that, if we should escape the ice, we immediately head south.

The request troubled me, but before I could answer, Frankenstein, who appeared not to have
10 enough strength to speak, addressed the crew. His voice was so persuasive and moderate that the men were moved and left my cabin. I turned to thank my friend, but he collapsed, almost dying on the spot.

15 How this will end, I don't know. I don't want to return to England without meeting my goal, but I am afraid the men cannot continue in the present hardships.

According to the passage, Frankenstein is about to

_____.

① die
② fight with the monster
③ return to England

ANS. ①

September 12th

It is decided. I am returning to England. My hopes are blasted by cowardice and indecision. I have lost my hopes of glory; I have lost my friend.

5   When the ice finally broke on September 9th the crew insisted on heading south. Frankenstein heard their shouts of joy and addressed me. "If you must abandon your goal, I will not abandon mine. I am weak, but the spirits of heaven who 10 guide me, will give me strength." He tried to get out of bed but collapsed. Before he died he begged me to complete his mission.

   Margaret, what can I say about such a sudden death? What can I say so you understand how sad 15 I am? But now I am interrupted. I hear a voice coming from where Frankenstein is lying. It is almost midnight and I must go see what it is. Goodnight, my sister.

blast 꺾다
cowardice [káuərdis] 겁, 소심
indecision 우유 부단
abandon 포기하다, 버리다
complete 완성하다, 완수하다
mission 임무, 사명

. . . .

2 My hopes are blasted by cowardice and indecision.
소심함과 우유부단함은 내 희망을 꺾어버렸다.

6 the crew insisted on heading south
선원들은 남쪽으로 향하기를 고집했다

14 What can I say so you understand
how sad I am?
내가 지금 얼마나 슬픈지 네가
이해하게 하려면 뭐라고 말해야 할까?

15 now I am interrupted
지금 난 (편지쓰는 것을)
중단해야겠다

'he begged me to complete
his mission'에서 밑줄 친 부분이
의미하는 것은?

① going to the North Pole
② killing the monster
③ being a great captain

ANS. ②

Great God! What a scene has just taken place! I entered my friend's cabin and over his body stood a huge creature that was distorted and horribly ugly. I turned my face from him but called on him
5 to stay.

He stared at me in disbelief for a moment then addressed his lifeless creator. "That is also my victim! In his murder, my crimes are complete. Oh Frankenstein! Generous and self-devoted human, I
10 ask you to forgive me. I destroyed you by destroying everything you love."

"Your repentance," I said, "is useless. If you would have listened to your conscience before you exacted your vengeance, Frankenstein would still be alive."

"Do you dream?" said the demon. "I heard 5 Clerval's groans as I took his life. I was heartbroken when I returned to Switzerland. I pitied Frankenstein and hated myself."

distorted 찌그러진, 일그러진   repentance 후회, 회개
disbelief 불신   conscience 양심
generous 관대한   groan[groun] 신음(소리), 불평
self-devoted 자기 희생적인   pity 불쌍히 여기다

· ·

1 What a scene has just taken place!
  이게 도대체 무슨 광경이란 말인가!
4 (I) called on him to stay 그에게 거기 있으라고 했다
6 He stared at me in disbelief
  그는 불신감으로 나를 바라보았다
  If you would have listened to your
  conscience before you exacted
  your vengeance
  복수를 하기 전에
  당신의 양심의 소리를
  들었더라면

이 장면에서 나타난 괴물의 심경은?

① regretful
② revengeful
③ angry

ANS. ①

"But when I discovered that he sought happiness with a woman but would not make a woman for me, I was filled with rage and a thirst for vengeance. I remembered my threat and decided to carry it out. Yet when she died I had no regrets. I had cast off all feelings and had no choice but to adapt my nature to a way it had not chosen. Now it is ended. There is my last victim."

At first I was moved by his words. Then I remembered what Frankenstein had said about his eloquence and persuasion. "You wretch. You are like someone who sets fire to a group of buildings and then after they are burned sits among the ashes and weeps. You hypocrite. You don't feel pity. You are just sorry that your victim is now beyond your power."

"It is not like that," interrupted the creature. "You call Frankenstein your friend so perhaps you

have some knowledge of my crimes. But the short time he spoke to you cannot compare with the months I endured
5 wrestling with passions that could never be realized."

eloquence 웅변, 능변
persuasion 설득(력)
hypocrite [hípəkrìt] 위선자
knowledge 앎, 지식

compare 비교하다
wrestle (일과) 씨름하다,
　　(문제 등에) 전력을 다하다
realize 깨닫다, 실감하다

· ·

4 I was filled with rage and a thrist for vengeance
　나는 분노와 복수에 대한 갈망으로 가득 찼소
7 decided to carry it out 그것을 실행하기로 결심했지
9 I had cast off all feelings and had no choice
　but to adapt my nature to a way it had not chosen.
　나는 모든 감정을 벗어버리고, 내 본성을 원치
　않는 모습으로 바꿔버리지 않을 수 없었소.
5 wrestling with passions that could
　never be realized 결코 실현될
　수 없는 열정을 실현하려
　무진장 애쓰면서

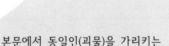

본문에서 동일인(괴물)을 가리키는
말이 <u>아닌</u> 것은?

① hypocrite
② creature
③ victim

ANS. ❸

"It is true that I am wretched. I have killed the harmless and the innocent. But don't worry. I will not do any more damage. My work is almost complete. The only death now required is my own. I won't be slow about it either. I will leave your ship and go as far north as I can. There I will build my funeral pile.

"Goodbye. You are the last human eyes I will see. Goodbye, Frankenstein! If you were still alive and still wanted revenge against me, it would be better taken in my life than my death. Although you were miserable, my agony was much greater.

"But soon," he cried with a sad enthusiasm, "I will die and what I feel will no longer be felt. My spirit will sleep in peace, or if it thinks, it will certainly not think this way. Goodbye."

He sprang from the cabin window and into his sled beside the ship. He was soon carried away by the waves and lost in darkness and distance.

---

wretched 야비한, 지독한   enthusiasm [enθúːziæzəm]
harmless 악의 없는, 순진한   열심, 열광
revenge 복수   darkness 어두움

· ·

1 I have killed the harmless and the innocent.
나는 악의 없는 사람들과 죄 없는 사람들을 죽였소.
6 (I will) go as far north as I can 가능한 한 멀리 북쪽으로 가겠소
2 what I feel will no longer be felt
내가 지금 느끼는 것(이 고통)도 더 이상 느껴지지 않을 거요
6 He was soon carried away by the waves and lost
in darkness and distance. 그는 곧 파도에 쓸려가
어둠 속으로 멀리 사라졌다.

'I will build my funeral pile'
이 암시하는 것은?

① 죽음
② 은둔
③ 복수

ANS. 1

Comprehension Checkup

I. 가족들이 죽고 난 후, Frankenstein이
취한 행동이 <u>아닌</u> 것은?

① He decided to leave Geneva forever.

② He decided to murder the monster.

③ He gave up his life.

2. 괴물이 잔인한 행동을 했던 근본적인 원인을 설명한 문장이다.
빈 칸에 들어갈 적절한 어휘를 고르시오.

People's _____ towards the monster made him do
evil things.

① indifference   ② prejudice   ③ worry

3. 다음 문장에 나타난 공통적인 감정은?

- I could smash in his cursed head.
- Call out the names of my family and ram your
  sword into his heart.
- Let the hellish monster drink deep of agony.

① anger   ② concern   ③ jealousy

4. 본문의 내용과 일치하지 <u>않는</u> 것은?

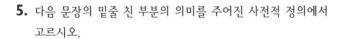

① Frankenstein asked Walton to
   revenge for him.
② The monster was murdered by Walton.
③ The monster repented what he had done.

5. 다음 문장의 밑줄 친 부분의 의미를 주어진 사전적 정의에서
고르시오.

You have read this strange and <u>terrific</u> story, Margaret.

> **terrific** *adj.* ① huge; intense ② excellent
> ③ causing terror

6. Frankenstein의 사망 원인은?

① 괴물에게 살해되어서
② 건강이 악화되어서
③ 굶주림으로 인해서

7. Frankenstein의 죽음 앞에서 괴물이 보인 행동이 <u>아닌</u> 것은?

① The monster asked for forgiveness from him.
② The monster was delighted at his death.
③ The monster left the human world forever.

정답은 p.129에

ANSWERS

● **Checkup I** (30~31쪽)

1. ①　　2. ②
3. ③　　4. ③
5. ③　　6. ①
7. ②
8. ①-ⓐ, ②-ⓒ,
　③-ⓓ, ④-ⓑ

● **Checkup II** (68~69쪽)

1. ③　　2. ②
3. ①　　4. ②
5. ③-①-②-④
6. ①　　7. ③

● **Checkup III** (102~103쪽)

1. ②　　2. ②

3. The monster

4. ①　　5. ①

6. ② 　7. ②

● **Checkup IV** (126~127쪽)

1. ③　　2. ②

3. ①　　4. ②

5. ③　　6. ②

7. ②

No story can be more tragic than this.
Frankenstein tried to create a new life,
with enthusiasm and excitement.
But it turned out to be an ugly monster.
He was horrified, so he deserted it.
The creature was left all alone,
with no friend in the world.

Listen to me, my creator.
I didn't mean to hurt them.
With prejudice in their eyes,
they only see how I look,
and don't see what I am.
So I am very lonely.
Since you are the one who made me,
you have to create my companion.

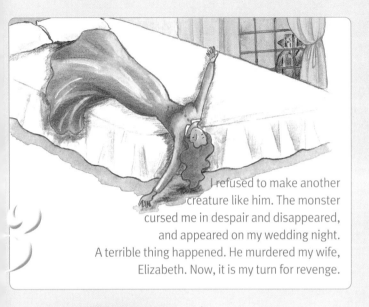

I refused to make another creature like him. The monster cursed me in despair and disappeared, and appeared on my wedding night. A terrible thing happened. He murdered my wife, Elizabeth. Now, it is my turn for revenge.

Death and revenge were endlessly repeated. It seemed that this tragedy would never end. Finally, Frankenstein collapsed and died. The monster was sad over the death of his creator, and sorry about what he had done. Then, he disappeared from people's eyes, forever. Since all the tragedy came from man's prejudice, the monster was also a victim.

Word List

다음은 이 책에 나오는 단어를 수록한 것입니다.
*표는 교육부 고시 교육과정에서 제시하는 기본 어휘입니다.

abandon 포기하다
absolutely* 절대적으로
accompany 함께 가다
account*
　…의 이유를 밝히다; 설명
accurately 정확하게
accuse* 고소하다
affectionate 애정어린
agitation 동요
agony 고민, 고통
amaze* 놀라게 하다
anguish 고통, 괴로움
anxious* 걱정하는,
　　　　갈망하는
apparently 명백하게
appearance 외모
approach* 접근하다
arrest* 체포하다
assure 보장하다
atmosphere* 분위기

attach* 붙이다
attack* 공격하다
avoid* 피하다

barren 불모의, 메마른
battle 전투, 싸움
belief 믿음
beloved 사랑하는
bitterly 쓰게, 몹시
blame* 비난하다
blood* 피
border 경제, 국경
brief* 간결한, 짧은
breath* 호흡
bury* 묻다, 매장하다

captain 선장, 기장
capture 붙잡다

carriage 탈 것, 수레
carve 조각하다
caution 조심, 경고
cemetery 묘지, 무덤
character* 특성, 인물
charge* 돌격하다
chase* 추격하다
chemistry 화학
chop 팍팍 찍다
claim* 주장하다
clearly 명백하게
coffin 관
collapse 실신하다
combine* 결합하다
comfort 위로, 위안;
　　　　위로하다
commit* 저지르다
companion 동료
compare* 비교하다
complain* 불평하다
complete* 완전한;
　　　　완성하다

concerned 걱정하는
condemn 비난하다
confess 실토하다
confidence 신용, 확신
confirmation 확정
conscience 양심
consider* 숙고하다
consist*

　　…으로 이루어져 있다
console 위로하다
constantly 변함없이
contempt 경멸, 모욕
contentment 만족
continue* 계속하다
convince 납득시키다
corpse 시체
court* 안뜰, 궁전, 법정
cowardice 소심, 겁
crack 갈라진 금, 틈
create* 창조하다
creature 생물, 피조물
crew 승무원, 선원
criminal 범죄자
criticize* 비난하다
cruelly 잔인하게
crush 눌러서 뭉개다
curious* 호기심 나는
current 현재의; 조류
curse 저주, 욕

damage* 손상, 손해
damp 축축한;

　　　습기, 안개
deadly 치명적인
decay 썩다
declare* 선언하다
dedicate 바치다
deed 행위, 실행
defect 결함, 결점
defense 방어, 수비
deformity

　　　기형, 모양이 흉함
delay* 지연시키다
delight* 기쁘게 하다
demand* 요구하다
deny* 부인하다
departure 출발, 떠남
depend 의지하다
depressing 울적해지는
descend* 내려가다
describe* 묘사하다
desert* 버리다; 사막
desire* 바라다;

　　　욕구, 욕망
despair 자포자기, 절망
despise 경멸하다

destiny 운명
destroy* 파괴하다
determined 단호한
devil* 악마, 사탄
devote* 바치다
disappearance 사라짐
disaster* 재난, 재앙
disbelief 불신
discover* 발견하다
disgust 혐오;

　　　싫증나게 하다
dismay 경악, 낙담;

　　　실망시키다
distinguished 출중한
distort 왜곡하다
disturb* 방해하다
dreadful 두려운
dreary 황량한, 울적한
due* 도착 예정인,

　　　…에 기인하는
duty* 의무

edge* 테두리, 날
edible 먹을 수 있는
educate* 교육하다
effect* 효과, 결과
effort* 노력

eloquence 능변

embrace 포옹하다

empty* 텅 빈

encourage* 격려하다

endure 인내하다

entire 전체의, 완전한

escape* 탈출하다

especially* 특히

eternal 영원한

evade 피하다

eventually 마침내

everlasting 영구한

evidence* 증거

exactly 정확하게

exceed 초과하다

exchange* 교환하다

exclaim 외치다

execute 실행하다

exist* 존재하다

expect* 기대하다

expedition 탐험

extinguish 끄다

extremely 극도로

faint* 기절하다

fatal 치명적인

fatigue 피로, 피곤

fiend 마귀, 악마

figure* 모양, 인물, 숫자

flee 도망치다

force* 힘, 폭력, 무력;
억지로 …시키다

forgive* 용서하다

frightening 무서운

fulfill 성취하다

funeral 장례식

fury 격노, 격분

gasp 헐떡거리다

gaze 응시, 주시; 응시
하다, 지켜보다

generous* 관대한

gigantic 거대한

grab 잡아채다

grateful* 감사하는

grave 무덤

gruffly 퉁명스럽게

guilty* 유죄의

hardly* 거의 …아니다

hardship 고난, 곤경

hasten 서두르다

haunt …에 자주 가다

horrible* 끔찍한

humanity
인류, 인간성, 인간애

hurl 집어던지다

hypocrite 위선자

hysterical
병적으로 흥분한

illness 질병

immediately 즉시

impulse 충동

increase* 증가하다

indecision 우유 부단

inedible 먹을 수 없는

inevitable 피할 수 없는

injury 부상, 상처

innocent 무죄인

inscription 명각, 비문

insist* 고집하다

inspire
…에게 영감을 주다

instantly 당장, 즉석에서

intend* …할 작정이다

interfere 간섭하다

interrupt* 가로막다

kneel 무릎을 꿇다
knowledge 지식

laboratory* 실험실
language* 언어
literature 문학
lonely* 외로운
long 간절히 바라다
loose* 느슨한, 헐거운

madness 광기
malicious 악의 있는
mankind 인류
marriage 결혼
melancholy 우울한
mention* 언급하다
merchant* 상인
miserable 비참한
misfortune 불운
mission 사명, 임무
mockery 비웃음
moderate 절제하는
murder 살해하다

nervous* 신경 과민한
notice* 알아차리다

obey* 순종하다
observation 관찰, 준수
obviously 명백히
occasionally 때때로
occupation*
　　　업무, 직업, 점유
overcome* 극복하다,
　　　압도하다

painfully 고통스럽게
passion 열정, 격정
peasant 농부, 소작인
permit* 허락하다
persecutor 박해자
persuade* 설득하다
philosophy 철학
playfully 장난스럽게
precaution 조심, 경계
prejudice 편견

present* 현재의,
　　　참석한; 선물
prevent 예방하다
previous* 이전의
pursue 쫓다, 추구하다

rapid 신속한, 빠른
reasonable 합리적인
reception 응접, 접대
recover* 회복하다
refuse* 거절하다
regarding …에 관하여
reject* 거절하다
release 풀어놓다
relieve 경감하다
repentance 후회
request* 요구;
　　　…에게 청하다
responsibility 책임
restless 침착하지 못한
resume 다시 시작하다
retire 은퇴하다
reveal* 드러내다
revenge 복수;
　　　복수하다
reward 보상
rob 빼앗다

satisfy 만족시키다
sacred 신성한
scheme* 계획, 설계
scholar 학자
scream 비명
secure 안전한;
　　　안전하게 하다
severely 호되게
slaughter 도살하다
smash 박살내다
snatch 잡아채다
sob 흐느껴 울다
solitude 외로움, 고독
soothe 위로하다
sorrow 슬픔
speculate 사색하다
spouse 배우자
stare 응시하다
starvation 굶주림
stubborn 완고한
stupid 어리석은
substitute 대용하다;
　　　대용물
successful 성공적인
suffer* (고통, 변화를)
　　　경험하다
supply* 공급; 공급하다

survive* 생존하다
swell 부어오르다
sympathize
　　　동정(공감)하다

telescope 망원경
tenderly 상냥하게
terrible 소름끼치는
terrific 무서운, 대단한
testimony 증언, 증거
threat* 위협
timid 겁 많은, 소심한
torment 고통, 고뇌
torture 고통;
　　　고문하다
tranquility 고요함
tremble 떨다

unbelievable
　　　믿을 수 없는
unconscious 무의식의
undisturbed
　　　방해받지 않은
uninhabited
　　　사람이 살지 않는

university* 대학
untrustworthy
　　　믿을 수 없는
urge 강력히 권고하다
utterly 아주, 전혀

vengeance 복수
virtually
　　　사실상, 실제적으로
voyage* 항해

wandering
　　　헤매는; 방랑
weep 울다
withstand
　　　(곤란 등을) 잘 견디다
witness 증언, 목격자
worried 걱정하는
wrap* 포장하다
wrestle
　　　(일과) 씨름하다,
　　　(문제 등에) 전력을 다하다
wretch 비열한 사람

Yellow Series · Pink Series

1,200단어 수준(Yellow Series),
2,800단어 수준(Pink Series)으로 분류하여 자신의
실력에 맞춰 골라 읽는 영어 소설 / 전 30권

사전 없이 읽는

세계 명작
영어 학습 문고

난이도에 따라 주니어편(♣), 초급편(★), 중급편(★★),
고급편(★★★)으로 나눈 문고의 스테디 셀러 / 전 80권

영한 대역 문고

학문적 깊이와 흥미를 만족시킬 수 있는 작품들만을 엄선해 원문과 함께
대역을 실어 준 세계 명작 고급편 / 전 100권

세계 명작 Spring Series 목록

영어로 읽는
세계 명작 스프링 시리즈

2000년 1월 5일 초판발행
2009년 1월 5일 인   쇄
2009년 1월 10일 중쇄발행

발행인 : 민 선 식

YBM)Si-sa

서울특별시 종로구 종로 2가 55-1
TEL (02) 2000-0515
FAX (02) 2271-0172

등록일자 : 1964년 3월 28일
등록번호 : 제 1-214호

인터넷 홈페이지 : http://www.ybmbooks.com